American Dreamer

American Dreamer

Lucid, Book 1

Christopher McMaster

Southern Skies Publications

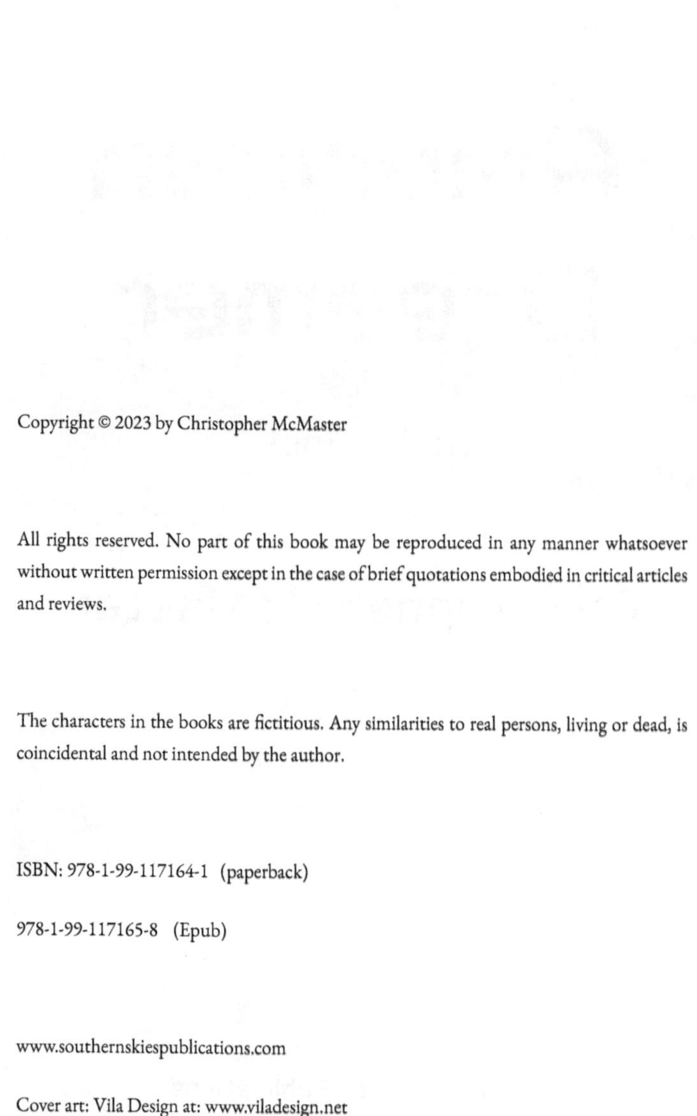

ISBN: 978-1-99-117164-1 (paperback)

978-1-99-117165-8 (Epub)

www.southernskiespublications.com

Cover art: Vila Design at: www.viladesign.net

For my parents, Ron and Donna, who would drag a young me in front of the TV news and make me watch history in the making. Well, this is how it really happens …

"What I understood, was that for better or worse, history was turned topsy turvy that night in Chicago ..."

Claude Pepper, American politician, member of the US Senate, 1936-1951

During the Democratic Party convention of 1944, party leaders knew they were not just choosing a vice president to serve alongside President Franklin Delano Roosevelt, but that they were deciding who would succeed him. The president was ill. Those close to him knew that, while he could win the next election, he would not survive his fourth term. Party leaders were choosing the next president, the man who would lead the country to an inevitable victory in the world war, as well as navigate the treacherous postwar world. The sitting vice president, Henry A. Wallace, was considered the second most popular man in the country. He represented the unions, black Americans, women, the voiceless, the unemployed. He championed what he called the *Century of the Common Man*. His vision of the world at permanent peace was one that did not celebrate an empire, and that did not promote militarism.

Party leaders found this intolerable. Instead, they manipulated the convention to ensure that a little known and more pliable candidate won the nomination. Seizing the podium before Wallace could be nominated, convention chairman Samuel Jackson called proceedings to halt, citing a fire hazard. Senator Claude Pepper was mere feet away when Jackson banged his gavel. That night, in preparation for the next day's deliberations, party bosses were able to chide and bribe and threaten enough convention delegates to vote their way. When President Roosevelt died in April, 1945, just weeks before Nazi Germany surrendered to Allied forces, Harry Truman was sworn in to replace him. Wallace was soon removed from the cabinet and retired to his farm in Iowa.

The party bosses got their way, as they usually do. They would even take credit for what happened that fateful night of July 20, 1944.

1

"*C*lose your eyes and relax. Just sit back, lie down if you want to. Tell me what you saw the first time you saw Miss Beil."

I was in a classroom. An old classroom. The first thing I noticed were the windows. They were square panes letting in a dirty light. I couldn't see anything outside them. I mean, it was as if the windows pointed up, into a cloud or something.

A long blackboard ran the length of the front of the room. That's what people called them back then. There was some writing on the board but I couldn't read it at first. It was like looking into water. I narrowed my eyes, squinting. It was a name or something. Her name.

There was a flag in the corner, on a pole mounted on the wall. It was an American flag, like what's in my classroom. I looked in the other corner, but that flag wasn't there.

I was sitting at a wooden desk. It was all one piece, the chair fixed to it, with only one way to get into it, sliding in from the left side. It had a lid that could lift and open. But I didn't open it. I stared at the surface. The wood was polished, rubbed smooth. But not with any kind of cleaner—more like years of fingers and hands using it.

That's when I saw my hands. I saw my own hands.

"Why were your hands so important?"

I looked at my fingers. That's how you can tell. It's a trick you can teach yourself."

"A trick for what?"

To know when you are dreaming. So you can be awake in your dreams. My nails were painted red. I did that with my mom a few days before. My nana's ring was on my finger. On my right hand, not the side when you're married. I always wear nana's ring. My mom's-mom's-mom. That's my great grandmother. It was a gold band with three small diamonds set in it. Most the time I have those stones turned over, on the inside. But they were facing up. I touched the ring with a finger on my left hand. Then I stared at my finger, my pointer finger.

"Your index finger."

I looked at the tip of my pointer finger. Then I put the tip of my finger on the desk, like I was pressing a button. That sounds stupid. I put my finger on top of the smooth wood of the desktop and pressed, slowly. I watched as my finger sank into the wood, first the tip, then the nail, up to my first knuckle. It didn't feel like much, just like it was being squeezed softly. I pulled my finger out just as slowly, and when it was all the way out I turned my finger and looked at it, just stared at it, like it wasn't mine or something, but I knew it was. I smiled. It seemed right somehow that I should be able to put my finger through wood.

I looked at the desk, which was just the same as before, and I put my whole hand on it, palm down. My hand sat there for a moment, and then I pressed down gently. I pressed until my entire hand had disappeared up to the wrist, all the time smiling all happy like.

Then I heard an almighty "whack!"—a sound that'd grow real familiar. I near jumped out of my seat. I blinked and saw my hand back on the desk--on it, not in it. I looked at where the sound came from and that's when I saw her for the first time.

"Who did you see?"

"I am Miss Beil and I will be your teacher," she said, looking me right in the eyes. "I would like to introduce a new member of the class. She has useful skills. I am sure you'll like her," she said. She had this soft drawl. 'Kantucky Talk', my mom would call it. My mom didn't like Kantucky. This Miss Beil stood at the front of the classroom, blonde hair flowing to her shoulders. She wore a white dress with black dots all over it, tied real tight at her tiny waist.

"Say hello to your classmates, Nadia," she said.

That's when I looked at the other desks for the first time. There were maybe fifteen more desks in the room, but only two had anybody sitting in them. One had a blonde white girl about my age. She was wearing some sort of old cheerleader outfit, a blue wide skirt and a sweater with a big letter 'R' on it. A white boy sat at the other desk. Real integrated room. It was the first time I was ever in a classroom with white kids. He had on dirty denim jeans that looked like they could stand up by themselves once he took them off his skinny legs. His shirt was, I don't know, plaid. Is that the right word? Lots of squares on it. Hipster or retro or something. Both were looking down at their desks, not even glancing my way. I didn't know then what they were so scared of.

"Hello," I said to their heads. I couldn't help it, but I started to giggle. It was all too weird.

And then, "whack!" Miss Beil had this wooden ruler in her hand. She had just hit it against her own desk, a big square block at the front of the class. She carefully laid the ruler down and sat beside it. She crossed her legs, all lady like, and smiled at us.

"As I said, you'll have a chance to meet each other later," she said in her soft drawl. "We have a lot to get through."

2

"Nadia, I need to ask you to open your eyes now."

Nadia blinked and looked across the room.

"I'm sorry I have to stop you, our time's almost up. Thank you for sharing today," he sounded sincere.

"What choice did I have?" Nadia shot back.

"Are you still taking your medication?" he asked, ignoring her question.

"What choice do I have?" Nadia repeated. Her tone was more resigned than resentful.

"You don't, I guess," he admitted. He became aware of his body language, uncrossed his arms, and sat up straighter in his chair. "The court order mandated our sessions, just like it does your medication..."

"The court order gives you the power to send me back, Mr. Foskett," Nadia interrupted.

"You can call me Michael," he answered. More approachable. She stared at him. "The order mandates I have to submit reports on your progress. That's all, just like I explained. If you don't talk, I don't have anything to report."

Nadia's stare turned into a glare.

"I'm really sorry, but I have to see you take your medication. You have it on you, right?"

"Don't I have to?"

"Yes. And I have to see you take it. It's mandated. We are both restricted by it." Michael Foskett prided himself on his patience, but it was growing increasingly thin. He crossed his legs and looked at the girl across the room. In a moment she would reach into her bag and take out a brown bottle with a white cap. She would remove the lid, shake out one of the white pills inside, and pop it into her mouth. They were his indispensable tag team buddies. Talking and pills. Especially pills, with cases like her.

Nadia swallowed the pill and showed him her pink tongue.

"Want one?" she asked.

"Are you still hearing the voices?" he responded.

"They aren't voices," she answered. She wasn't smiling anymore.

"When the police brought you in you were very distraught. You told the police, '*she* made me do it.' Is 'she' Miss Beil?" He had studied the police report as part of her referral file. He could picture Nadia in custody, terrified and shocked by where she was and what she had done.

"Cassy," Nadia said. "She lets us call her Cassy."

Nadia shifted her gaze from the man across from her, to the practice certificate above his desk, Chicago State University, Department of Psychology. The faded inspirational picture on the wall, a picture of the rocky mountains with a syrupy quote in gold letters at the bottom. She looked at the worn desk, and tried to ignore his writing on a pad of yellow paper, a new nugget of information. "Cassy."

"Is Cassy speaking to you now?" he asked. "Are you still hearing the voices?"

"They aren't voices," she said.

He raised his eyebrows, "the medication will stop the voices, Nadia."

"I don't hear voices in my head," she said. "I just told you about a dream, not voices in my head."

"And dreams are real, while the voices aren't?"

"Yes, they are. Shit. You make me sound crazy. I ain't crazy."

Nadia and her therapist sat in silence. Finally, he picked up a folder from his desk, opened it and scanned a page.

"Nadia, the psychiatrist who assessed you while you were in custody diagnosed you with paranoid schizophrenia. It's the only thing that has kept you out of prison. Or worse. Schizophrenia is an illness where a person can't tell what is real and what is not real. Voices and dreams seem real."

"Dreams are real!"

"And that's why we're both here now," he said. "The medication should stop you hearing, or dreaming, the voices."

"Fuck you!"

"Nadia, please!" he winced as if being struck. Just another day at the office. Another unwanted case assigned to his overloaded schedule.

He looked at the clock on the wall and moved his chair back. "I'm sorry, but we've gone over today. You may be late to school, and for that I apologize. I'll write a note accepting all blame." He opened a desk drawer, removed a letterhead. As he finished Nadia stood up, strode forward, took the note from his hand and left without saying another word.

"I'll see you next week," he said to the closing door.

Nadia walked down the stairs to the street below. She opened the door and for a moment thought about turning left. She was late anyway. What did she have to lose? She looked at the note and saw that Foskett had written the time on it.

"Prick!" she muttered. She saw the date was written poorly, easy to alter for future use, if she was able to keep hold of it. Small consolation. She turned right and caught the bus to 79th Street. It was waved through the Wentworth checkpoint and she arrived at Roosevelt High School.

She didn't recognize the guard at the first set of doors. All he did was direct her to the second. There they were more attentive. One took her bag and rifled through the contents. He took out the bottle of pills, read the label, and put it back with a smirk before putting the bag through the scanner. The other guard read Foskett's note, looking up with recognition after reading her name. He folded the note and handed it back to her, silently motioning to the full body scanner. She entered, raised her hands just like the yellow figure on the wall told her, and watched the bar rotate around. When the guard indicated she stepped out on the other side.

"Welcome to school," he said.

She glanced at him, appreciating the sarcasm. She smiled for the first time since Foskett's office that morning. She walked forward, down the tiled corridor, walking on the third tile from the wall, as per school rules. She turned a corner and walked down another corridor. Finally, she stood in front of a door with the number 12B on it. Civics and Citizenship. She lost her smile, assumed an expression of haste, and entered.

"Nadia. You're late."

"Sorry, Mr. Johnson, sir. I have a note ..."

"The class has said their morning pledge. As you missed it, why don't you do it now," her teacher said, ignoring the paper in her hand. She folded the note and put it into a pocket.

Nadia faced the front of the classroom where a flag stood in each corner. She angled her body to the left towards the US flag. She raised an outstretched hand, keeping her arm straight, but before her teacher could detect any mockery, she quickly bent her elbow and placed her hand over her heart. Her dad taught her that one. 'Funny how this,' he said, 'is just an elbow bend away from this.'

"I pledge allegiance to the flag of the United States of America and to the republic for which it stands, one nation under God, indivisible, with liberty and justice and all."

"Take your seat, Nadia," her teacher said.

Nadia sat at her desk. She heard the whispers start behind her, whispers she tried to ignore, but never could. The best she could do was to pretend not to hear.

"She's a radical like her old man ..."

"I heard she was in the Negro Liberation Movement ..."

"NLM? Wouldn't surprise me ..."

"Terrorist ..."

The whispers were silenced by the teacher. "Before we were interrupted, we were discussing the 29th Amendment, or at least trying to. These village idiots didn't know what it was," Mr. Johnson looked at Nadia.

"Nadia?" he asked.

"Executive Orders, sir," Nadia answered slowly. She was trapped, as usual. Mr. Johnson did not help Nadia make any friends, if that was even remotely possible anymore. He knew that she was his only student who had any chance of answering any of his questions.

"And what can you tell the village about Executive Orders, Nadia?"

"A president's Executive Orders can override both the judicial and the legislative branches of the government to—"

"To ensure the operational efficiency of the government," he interrupted. "Thank you, Nadia, who has bothered to read the text," Mr. Johnson sat down on his desk, "and why, class, was this amendment necessary?" The students continued to look blankly at their teacher while he continued to look at Nadia. She didn't wait to be asked.

"Because," she said, raising her voice, "the Executive resented checks and balances and wanted more power for himself."

Mr. Johnson stopped her by banging his palm on his desk. "That might be the type of subversive slander your father would write, and we know where that got him. But no, the 29th Amendment was, class, passed to ensure that one branch of government did not use its powers to cripple the country with inertia ...."

Mr. Johnson stopped and looked at his class with undisguised disgust. He ignored Nadia's sullen expression. "*Inertia,* class, is a tendency to do nothing. It is the enemy of progress. Now, what were the situations where Congress, *for example,* would try to cripple the country?"

He waited a moment before adding his usual prefix. "It's in your reading."

Bored with the silence he asked, "Nadia?"

"I don't know, sir," she lied.

Mr. Johnson glared at her. "Budgets! Budgets, class. Paying hand-outs to slackers and shirkers, known as *welfare*. And funding the military, the brave men and women that keep us safe and protect our freedoms."

He wiped spit from the corner of his mouth and continued with his lesson, but Nadia let his voice drone on in the background. When the other students stood signaling the end of class, she stood with them, and turned to face the flag in the right corner of the room. Eyes went to the white banner with the blue square and red cross. Hands went to hearts.

"All together!" Mr. Johnson barked.

Voices spoke in unison, "I pledge allegiance to the Christian flag and to the savior for whose kingdom it stands, one savior crucified risen and coming again with life and liberty to all who believe ..."

"Dismissed."

4

At the last bell Nadia filed out of school, along with hundreds of other students. When she reached the street, she was quickly herded in the direction of her bus. She sat silently during the short ride down 83rd to Ashland. She hopped off and looked at the checkpoint blocking her way home. Red and white striped wooden barriers, a couple of simple sawhorses. Not strong enough to stop a car, but the automatic rifles the two bored men in black carried could. Nadia approached slowly, glancing at the black Humvee parked behind them. The back door was open. A lot of girls got 'questioned' in those.

Nadia reached into her blouse and pulled out the cross, letting it hang visibly on her chest.

"Look what we have here, a bit of brown sugar to sweeten our coffee," said one.

Nadia smiled at him. Best to be pleasant. She read the patch on his shirt, Dark Stream Security. They weren't the worst. S-Os, so called 'safety officers'. Private armies patrolling the streets with license to kill.

"Step right up, sweetie. Let's see what you have in that bag," he said. He took her bag and tossed it to his partner.

"And now let's see what you might have on you," he added smiling.

Nadia raised her hands as he approached. He ran his hands down her arms, under her shoulders and slowly over her breasts. His hands continued downward, over her hips and to her ass, where one lingered for an uncomfortable moment. He patted the outside of her thighs, then moved to the inside and slowed down, feeling the warmth between her legs. He then slid his hands down to her ankles. His eyes never left hers.

"You have your ID, sweetie?" he asked.

Nadia handed her card over. He looked at it, and back at her. "What kind of foreign name is Ifedi?" he asked.

Nadia read the guard's name tag. "What kind of foreign name is Moretti?" Nadia responded.

The guard's face lost its smile, but the man with Nadia's bag interrupted any response. "Look what we have here!" he said, raising a brown bottle of pills. "She's got a couple of these. Says here on the label they're ... Chlor-pro-ma ..."

"Chlorpromazine," Nadia said. "They're my meds, all of them."

The pair looked at her blankly.

"They're anti-psychotics," she said. "For schizophrenia. Crazy pills."

The guard in front of her took a small step back. Nadia took her chance. She looked past the guards.

"Just keep your mouth shut! Don't talk to them," she said.

"Get out of my head! Leave me alone!" she shouted.

"They're already dead, they're dead-men-walking. Just like Englewood!"

The guards gripped their rifles tightly at mention of the name, the site of a rare Liberation Movement ambush where several S-O were killed. One pointed his rifle at Nadia. The other took a step backward and looked around nervously, moving the point of his rifle with his gaze. The two immediately felt outnumbered and exposed.

"Leave me alone!" Nadia shouted to an empty patch of sky.

"They're already dead," Nadia said, now looking at the guards.

"Give her the fucking bag," said Moretti. He grabbed the bag from his partner and shoved it into Nadia's arms. "Get the fuck out of here, psycho!" he said, pushing her past the roadblock.

Nadia knew she had a rifle pointed at her back as she continued down the street. She kept walking, eyes forward, until she turned onto Hermitage. She took a few deep breaths and slowed down. After a short distance she stepped off the sidewalk at a red brick house and walked up the broken concrete stairs to the door. She carefully opened the door, and dropped her bag onto the floor. She wanted to fall down next to it, but made it to the couch.

"Roadblocks give you any hassle?" her mother asked from the kitchen.

"Not more than usual," Nadia answered.

"I'd ask how your day was, but it don't look like I have to," her mother wiped her hands on a dish towel and came into the front room. She looked down at her daughter.

"I told the psych about a dream," Nadia said. "The first one."

"Well, that's OK," her mother said. "You have to tell him something."

"He's an imbecile," Nadia said.

"Yeah, well, right now he's got the power," she walked over to Nadia's bag. "Did you pick up your prescription?" she asked.

"It's inside," Nadia answered.

Her mother opened the bag and took out two full bottles of Chlorpromazine. She walked to the bathroom, lifted the toilet lid and emptied the contents into the bowl. Nadia listened to the flush. Her mother returned to the kitchen and filled the medicine bottle with small white mints.

"Just give him what he wants, it's the only way to buy some time," her mother said. "Now come over here, you need a hug."

5

I was sitting at my desk, looking at the smooth wood surface. I put my hand on it, and was going to press down when I heard Miss Beil. "It's time we began our class," she said.

And then she was standing next to me. I don't know how she got there. I blinked and she was standing next to me. She put her hand on mine and I flinched. Her touch was cold.

"We don't have time for games right now, Nadia."

"Your dreams seem very real to you, Nadia," Foskett interrupted.

"I told you, they are real. I go to sleep, but then I wake up, in my dreams. And everything is real," Nadia said.

"*Seems* real, do you mean?" Foskett tried.

"Have you ever been hurt in a dream? Really hurt? You don't worry about what is real or not when you're in pain. You just know it hurts."

"Does Miss Beil hurt you?" Foskett asked.

"Not any more. No. She doesn't."

"She stopped hurting you?" he asked. Foskett took his yellow notepad and jotted something down.

"That's what I just said," Nadia answered.

"There is a type of dream called lucid, where you become aware that you are dreaming," he said. "Your dreams sound very lucid."

"Whatever."

"It's where you actually *notice* that you are in a dream. Something might trigger this awareness, like when you noticed your hands. That told you you were in a dream."

"OK," Nadia looked at the ceiling.

"It sounds like you are still having these dreams, Nadia. Your medication should be stopping them."

He set the notepad back on his desk and looked at her from across the room. She took three slow breaths as she looked back.

"I'm telling you about dreams I had. I'm not dreaming anymore," she lied.

"That's good," he said. "You have to let me know if they start again, Nadia."

"Like I was saying, Miss Beil was standing next to me."

And then she wasn't there, but standing in front of the classroom, speaking in that Kantucky drawl but sort of monotone. No expression.

"As I was saying, class," she said, "there's a war going on out there, right out that door, nation fighting nation, great battles fought for garbage, but in the final battle the winner will find themselves the losers and the losers even worse than lost. That is the only fight that matters, that battle planned eons ago and the one you will play a part in ..."

"I don't understand what you are saying, Nadia," Foskett said.

"I know you don't understand," Miss Beil said, "and maybe you never will, it doesn't matter one iota. What matters is that you are here now in this classroom so you can learn your lessons and grow up to be fine young citizens protecting their present and never shirking, never shirking, and doing just as you are told."

She sat on top of her big desk and crossed her arms. "Things don't work out the way they do accidentally," she said. "The world leader who gets assassinated. The prophet who dies on the road. The breakthrough invention. Have you ever wondered why a baby might just die one night?

Have you ever thought about who they would have grown up to be, or what they might have achieved? No, you probably haven't."

The soles of her shoes slapped the floor as she hopped off the desk. "And I'll tell you this: sometimes there is somebody there, somebody just like you, doing as they're told, by somebody like me. But you won't be killing any babies or prophets, nothing as fun as that. No, it's something much easier. You're going to help make sure a president gets elected. You'll do as I say, and you'll make sure your own present comes to fruition, a present of God fearing, or just fearful, fine citizens. It's a future I find quite rewarding. But," she said, "You will each have to do your part."

Miss Beil stopped talking as suddenly as she began. I looked down at my desk and shook my head. When I looked up again Miss Beil was standing beside the cheerleader. The cheerleader was staring at the surface of her desk. It looked like she was trying to get as far from Miss Beil as the wooden desk would allow. But she was trapped. Miss Beil reached down and ran her fingers through the cheerleader's blonde hair. The cheerleader sat completely still.

"I need to spend some time with June today, so you two can go and play. Why don't you go outside and explore the city a bit?" She said it as a question, but it was clear that it wasn't. She wasn't even looking at us as she spoke, she just stared down at June. I slowly got up and stood beside my desk. The white boy in the dirty denim jeans did the same.

"Off you go now," Miss Beil said without turning, fingers entwined in June's hair.

I looked at the white boy and then at the door. We both walked towards it. He got there first and pushed. The door swung open and we stepped outside.

"Holy shit!" I said.

He grabbed my arm before I stepped clear off the sidewalk and into the street. A green and white bus passed in front of me and I just stood and stared at it. Electric lines ran down the street. The bus had long poles that stretched up to touch the cables. People walked past, women in dresses and men in suits. One shoved me hard. "Out of the way, girl!" he said.

I was about to shout back, but that white boy still had hold of my arm and he pulled me the other way.

"Just be quiet and keep walking," he whispered.

I pulled my arm loose but did as he said. He walked to the first corner and turned right. He kept glancing back to make sure I was there, but I was way too stunned to think of doing anything other than following. I must have looked like a fish, my mouth open and eyes wide. Another green and white bus rushed by. Cars honked. Old cars, classic cars, like out of an old movie. A soldier in an old uniform walked past us, followed by some sailors. I giggled at their costumes. Men with straw hats and fancy suits, ladies in floral or striped dresses. Everybody looked very well dressed. They looked like they were on their way some local theatre production rehearsal. I bumped into the white boy and he grabbed my shoulders.

"You have to calm down, Nadia. This is serious. We have to get somewhere quiet." He sounded serious, so I became serious too. I followed him quietly, watching the people and the cars. I saw a man in a doorway, sitting on a piece of cardboard. Now that was something I was used to. He looked back at me, right back at me, and opened his mouth, I don't know, to say something or just gape, but then the white kid pointed to a blue sign sticking out from a building and headed straight for it. The sign said, 'Lunch.'

He pushed open a glass door and we went to a long counter where a woman with an apron leaned. It was a diner, with seats at the counter and booths all along one wall. He grabbed my arm and squeezed it. A waitress led us to both at the rear of the diner.

"Coffee?" she asked the white kid. She didn't glance my way, or ask what I wanted.

"Yes, please," he said. "Two, please."

The waitress came back with two cups of coffee. She dropped two menus on the table. "I'll be back in a moment," she said to the boy as she walked away.

"She won't," he said. "I'll have to go up when we're ready to order."

"What the hell is going on?" I asked him.

"What? Oh ... it's just how things are. Calm down."

"What do you mean, how things are? *Did you see how she treated* us?*"*

"Treated you, Nadia. *Where do you think you are?"*

I just glared at him, then I looked around the diner again. A bunch of white folks eating.

"A better question would be, 'when do you think you are?'" He pulled a few dollar bills out of his pocket and put them in front of me. "She sometimes leaves them on my desk. It usually means she wants me to leave the room. They go a long way around here."

He picked one up and stood. "I'll just order sandwiches."

When I was alone at the table, I looked closer at some of the bills he left on the table. They were crinkled and green. But they looked different than now. President Washington still on the front. It said, 'Silver Certificate' above him. I squinted at the small print. 'One dollar in silver payable to bearer on demand,' it said. I looked at the right side and in small letters it had a date. 1935.

He came back carrying two plates and a newspaper under one arm. He put one of the plates in front of me.

"There is *a war on. Not that stuff Miss Beil was talking about. God knows what that was all about, she tends to ramble at times. We just*

invaded France. Our boys are pushing on to Cherbourg. Here, look," he pointed at the date on the newspaper.

It said, Monday, June 12, 1944. I looked at the headlines.

"Yanks Gaining in Three Drives," it read.

"Pastors Beg Divine Help in Invasion."

"Tank Cannon Blasts Nazis out of Trees."

He was smiling at me. "My name is Randall," he said.

"Randall," I repeated. I looked at the diners again. The men sitting at the counter bent over their food. The waitress pouring coffee for three women sitting in a booth. Two men in uniforms watching them from their stools.

"Why are we here, Randall?" I asked.

"We're here because she wants us to be here. Why, though—I don't know yet. Like she said, something about the president. But she has a reason," Randall answered. "She always does."

6

R *andall took a bite of his sandwich. "I love ham on rye," he said.*

"Who is she, Randall?" I asked.

"No one to be treated casually, as she would say. And she isn't. I was surprised you got away with giggling. Has she given you a test yet?" Randall asked.

"Test?"

"Obviously not. A task, an exercise, to help ... train you. Make you obedient."

"I don't know what you're talking about," I said.

"Of course you don't. But you will. She's probably giving June her test now. Or talking about her progress," he took another bite of his sandwich.

"I still don't know what you're talking about," I repeated.

"You will. She'll give you a test and you'll have to do it. Everybody has to sleep. And that's why you'll do it. Or you'll regret it. After your test you'll just do what she tells you. It's for the best. I don't know. It's like she gets her power by things working out the way they do. 'Creating a reality,' she calls it. And she needs our help."

"Bullshit."

"Real shit."

"You had your test and now you're all scared of her?"

Randall paused and swallowed. He took a drink of coffee, "I did what she told me. And I do what she says."

"What was it? What did she tell you do?" I asked.

It took him a moment to answer. "I had to start a fire."

"Is that it?"

"No, that's not it. I had to start a big fire, in a beautiful ancient temple. She said, 'burn it to the ground, Randall, to ensure your present comes to pass,' and that is what I did. I didn't want to, I tried not to, but she made me in the end," he toyed with his sandwich, pushing it across his plate.

"She made *you?" I asked.*

"You'll understand," he said. "Do you have a nightmare? An absolute fear? I hope you don't, I really do. Because she'll find it, and she'll use it. But we all do somewhere deep down." His eyes met mine.

"My nightmare is fire," he said.

He turned to the side and slowly lifted his shirt. His entire torso and chest were scarred. "I hate fire," he said. "My parents died in the fire that burned me. I can't think of a worse nightmare. That's why she made me do it. She said, 'burn the temple, make it burn to protect our present.' So I burned the temple. And the nightmares went away. Protecting our present. She is always saying that. I don't have a present worth protecting. But I burned her temple anyway. You should have seen it. We have pictures of ruins and things, of where cities used to be. You look at this temple now and all you see are a few columns on the ground. Except one. One column still standing with a god damned stork nest or something on top of it. But not that day. Not when I saw it.

"So you burned it down?" Nadia asked.

"I did what she told me to. She has her reasons. Sometimes we just don't understand them. And she knows your nightmare, so you do what she says. I had to slip in with the worshippers and find a spot out of the

way, somewhere behind the statue. I had as many sticks and handfuls of straw hidden under my cloak as I could carry. I started a little fire. Have you ever tried to start a fire with a flint? No matches or lighter, just flick flick flick. It took me two tries. Twice I had to go back. But it caught, and spread up the walls and then to the roof."

We just sat silently after that, eating our sandwiches.

"We shouldn't hang around too long. Let's get out of here," he finally said. He took another bite of his sandwich, finished his coffee and stood up. He reached into his pocket and emptied the change on the table.

"You are not seriously leaving a tip for her?" I asked.

"There's no point in holding onto it. It's not like I'll wake up with it. Check 'em out. Indian Head nickels." He picked one up and handed it to me. I turned it over and saw a buffalo. United States of America. Five cents. I looked at the waitress and placed it back onto the table. Randall made his way to the door, smiling at her as he passed, "thank you very mu ch."

Outside we squinted in the bright light. I stood against the building to let people pass.

"Look familiar?" Randall asked.

"No," I said.

"The buildings are just older. It's the same city. Try harder," he said.

Brick and stone buildings lined the street. Awnings stretched over the sidewalk. Signs glowed neon. Billiards and Pool. Hillmann Boston Store. Dentist. A long sign was running down the side of a brown building, lit up with hundreds of light bulbs: Hotel Planters.

"That white tower over there, see? Over the roofs? That's the Wrigley Building. You can't see its clock from here," Randall said. "The good old Windy City."

We just stood there, watching people walk up and down the street, everybody having some place to go and something to do.

"Sometimes they notice, like they know, somehow," Randall said.

"What are you talking about?" I asked.

"Sometimes it's like they know we aren't from here. That homeless guy in the doorway on the way to the cafe. Did you notice him? I think he knew. Something in the way he looked at us," he moved his head slightly to the right, "and that guy there, smiling at us and pretending not to be looking. The one that looks like he cut his own hair."

A white guy holding a hat was leaning against a signpost about fifty feet down the street. His hair was cut close to his scalp.

"Let's move on, OK? Just find a quieter place." We walked maybe three or four blocks, turning left, then right. Randall checked over his shoulder every few steps. He finally stopped at a small square lined by trees. He checked over his shoulder again and sat on a nearby bench.

"I am going to close my eyes now. You should do the same," he said. I looked at him blankly.

"You don't know much, do you?" he said. "Find a quiet spot, close your eyes, and drift off. Go home. Wake up."

I sat down next to him.

"Might as well be here," he said. He stretched out his legs and leaned back. He smiled at me, and closed his eyes. I watched the wind blow through the trees above us, listened to the birds for a moment, and did the same.

7

I was at school again, in the classroom. It was quiet, but not empty. June was sitting at her desk, and Randall at his. They were looking down as usual. The long chalk board stood in front of the room, the teacher's desk in the middle. Miss Beil wasn't there. I waited for her to come in, but she didn't. Just me and June and Randall.

Nadia was more used to the weekly routine, starting the week with a visit to her therapist. She came in, sat on the worn couch, and after a few moments of silence would close her eyes and start to talk.

"How has it been at school, Nadia?" Foskett was sitting with his yellow notepad in his lap.

Nadia opened her eyes but didn't respond.

"I have to speak to your teachers from time to time. They say you don't have any friends, that you keep to yourself a great deal," he said.

"The crazy violent girl. Who wants to hang with that?" Nadia asked.

"I am told that the others can be quite cruel," he said.

"Whatever," Nadia answered.

"Your teachers seemed to have the impression that you would rather be somewhere else," he tried again.

"Who wouldn't?" Nadia said. "Stuck in a room lorded over by some adult, and made to learn shit you'll never use let alone remember. All you learn in school is how to do as you're told."

"And isn't that an important lesson?" Foskett asked.

"Yeah," Nadia answered. "Sure."

"We all have to do as we're told," he said.

"You're starting to sound like Miss Beil," Nadia said. "And Randall. And June."

"Would you call June and Randall your friends?"

Nadia sat silently, avoiding the trap. *So, you're still having the dreams?*

"You were telling me about a dream when you were alone in the classroom with June and Randall," he said.

"I was," Nadia answered.

I couldn't see Miss Beil, just her big empty desk in the front of the room. June and Randall sat there real still, looking down at the space in front of them. I walked to the front of the room to where Miss Beil's desk was. June spoke up. She just kept her head down and said real serious: "you need to stay at your desk."

I stared at her until she made eye contact.

"Miss Beil ain't here," I said to her.

"Miss Beil is always here," she said.

"Nadia, sit down," Randall said. He sounded worried.

I ignored them and stood over Miss Beil's desk. It was a solid old thing. There was a drawer in the middle. I had a strong urge to open the drawer and see what was inside, but June and Randall staring at me with their wide eyes gave me the creeps. I reached down and touched the desk. I put my finger on it and pressed gently. The tip slowly disappeared into the wood. I removed it and placed my palm flat on the surface, sinking it slowly.

"Nadia! Don't! She might come in!" Randall hissed.

I lifted my hand and turned away from Miss Beil's desk.

"So, where is she?" I asked. I sat at a desk in front of theirs.

"I don't know." It was June who answered. She was really pretty. It was the first time I'd had a good look at her. "She's always here. I think we should just wait."

"Man, you are scared of her," I said.

She lowered her head.

"She give you a test June? When me and Randall went out? What'd you have to do?" I asked.

June's eyes got wet, like she was going to cry. A tear ran down her cheek and she wiped it with the sleeve of her sweater, the one with the big R on it. She spoke real soft, I had to lean in to hear.

"She told me what she wanted," June said. "What I had to do."

"And? What did she want?"

"I don't have to tell you," she said. She raised her head to look at me. "Why don't you just behave yourself so we don't all get punished!"

I didn't know what she meant, but it was pretty clear she wasn't going to talk to me anymore. I opened my hands and shrugged. Randall looked at me and shook his head. I got up and went back to my desk, sat down and watched the front of the empty class. A clock on the wall ticked. June and Randall went back to looking at their desks.

Miss Beil never came in. I closed my eyes.

8

"The last time you were here, you said you closed your eyes. Is that how you wake up, Nadia?"

"That's how I would wake up. Most of the time." Nadia was still careful about her use of tenses. The sooner Foskett thought she was dream free, the closer she might be to some sort of freedom. "In the beginning I think things just sort of faded out. But later I would close my eyes, yeah. Like on the bench with Randall. But ..."

Foskett sat silently across from Nadia. He took a sip from a mug of coffee, setting it down carefully.

"But?" he asked.

"But ... sometimes that didn't work. And once Miss Beil ... it's hard to describe." Nadia shifted on the couch. "She kind of, used her hands ..."

"She touched you?" Foskett asked.

"Not like that," Nadia said. "It's ... I don't quite know what happened. I didn't like it."

"Can you tell me about it?"

She came into class and was steaming. We could tell she was angry. She was still in control, but there was this tense energy all around her that seemed to build up. She had her wooden ruler in one hand and was slapping it noiselessly in the other. She walked up to her desk and looked at it, and then she looked at me. All that angry energy focused on me.

"Someone has been a naughty girl, not doing what she should," Miss Beil said.

June and Randall were sitting like stones, eyes down at their desks. My eyes went down as well. I felt Miss Beil in front of me, could see the bottom of her dress, standing there for the longest moment tapping that ruler in her hand. White dress full of black spots.

And then she was gone, and standing next to June. There was a swishing sound, wood cutting through air, followed by an almighty "smack". I looked over and June had a thick red welt across her face. June looked confused, but then the pain registered. Tears welled up in her eyes and her hands went to her face, cradling the raw skin. She didn't make a noise, she just sat there holding her face in her hands, shaking slightly as she tried not to cry. Miss Beil leaned down and whispered something into June's ear. June's eyes grew wide and she tilted her head to look at Miss Beil, but Miss Beil wasn't looking at her. She was staring at me.

"June and Randall will be leaving us today," she said. "Nadia and I have something to discuss."

June and Randall got up from their desks and made their way to the door. I listened to the door close and knew I was alone with Miss Beil. She leaned against a desk and smiled.

"Nadia. My Nadia," she said. "I've been waiting for this little chat. I am so happy we get to have it today." She looked at me smiling.

"Do you know what we're going to talk about?" she asked.

"My test?" I answered.

"Good girl. I am sure Randall and June have told you about our tests. Randall was a good boy and completed his. He passed with flying colors. But then again, all he had to do was set his family house on fire. A little boy playing with matches. These things happen. And he has been

the model student ever since, setting a fire wherever I ask him to," she was still smiling and talking pleasant like, but the smile wasn't real. I gripped my desk.

"And June. Dear June. She is having a little trouble, but I am certain she will succeed. She's not the brightest spark, but she's useful. She is a very pretty young thing, don't you think?"

I knew she didn't want an answer.

"Now you, my warrior, you have your own uses. I saw that on your first day. For you, I have a special test, something very important for you to do."

She stood up and walked to her desk. She looked at me as she opened the middle drawer and took out a plain wooden handle. She held it in her hand and then flicked her wrist. There was a sharp click as a long blade folded out and locked into place.

"Such a useful tool.," she turned the knife in her hand, looking down the length of the blade. She touched the edge carefully with her thumb.

"Randall has his matches, June has her looks, and you, Nadia, have a knife," Miss Beil walked towards me with the blade in front of her. "Do you like knives, Nadia?"

"Not really," I told her.

"It doesn't matter, actually," she stood over me. "Show me your palm, Nadia. Turn your hand over."

I let go of the desk and did as she said. She put her free hand over my wrist and held it still. I wanted to pull it away, but couldn't. I couldn't move at all. I couldn't speak at all. All I could do was sit and watch as she took the knife and ran the blade gently across my palm. It was a simple motion. All I felt was a smooth, cold touch. I looked down. There was a thin pink line running across my hand. It became darker red as the blood welled to the surface and spread into my palm. She continued to hold my wrist as a few drops spilled onto my desk.

Then she let go. I grabbed my palm with my other hand as the pain started to register.

"A sharp blade is an object of beauty. It gives such a sweet kiss," Miss Beil said. She lay the knife on my desk and leaned back on the desk behind her.

"It's yours," she said, nodding towards the knife. "It's what you'll use. But first you have to pass your test. So I know that you will do what you have to when the time comes."

I opened my mouth but couldn't speak.

"There is a man I want you to visit," she went on. "When you wake up, find him, and cut him. With a knife. Simple really."

She took a finger and tapped her ear. "Just listen, now," she said. "You're going to wake up and look for this man. You won't have trouble finding him. You'll find a knife, a beautiful sharp one like this. And you'll cut him."

"He's a bit of a troublemaker, you'll be doing us all a favor," she added. She raised her eyebrows.

"You want me to kill somebody?" I said. "You're crazy."

"You weren't listening. And no, this isn't about crazy, it's about loy-alty."

"Well, I ain't killing nobody," I told her.

She picked the knife up off the table. She leaned close to me and pressed the flat of the blade against my cheek. She lightly patted my face with the blade. Once. Twice. Three times. I tried to shrink away from it, but couldn't move. She smiled even more.

"What I asked you to do was to cut him. Send him a message. Killing would only be a bonus," she said. "Call it, 'extra credit'."

She set the knife down and put her hands over mine. When she lifted them they were coated in my blood. She looked at her red hands and turned them for me to see. Then she reached out and took my face in those hands. She put one hand over my eyes, squeezed hard and said: "Nadia, you have work to do. Listen close. His name is Jones. Glasses. Real handsome man. He works in the city. Find him and cut him."

She squeezed even harder and pushed my head back and shouted, "Nadia, wake up!"

I opened my eyes and saw my room. My mom was sitting next to me, holding my head in her hands. I screamed and shook loose. I looked at my hand, the smooth skin of my palm. No cut, no blood. All I could do was lie there and cry.

"Did your mom know about what you were going to do?" Foskett asked.

"Don't bring my mom into this, she didn't know nothing, nothing at all," Nadia said.

"You never told your mom about your dreams?"

"No. Not at all. I told that to the police. All she knew was that I had nightmares and that I would wake up screaming."

Nadia watched as Foskett wrote on his notepad. He flipped over a page and kept writing.

9

*J*une and Randall came out of the school building and walked up a wide street. The downtown skyline lay ahead, looming closer as they walked. Brownstone apartments gave way to store fronts. June watched the women in their tailored dresses, heeled shoes and handbags. She self-consciously crossed her arms in front of her sweater. A woman passed her and frowned, glancing at the welt on the side of her face and then at the young man she was following.

"Where are we going?" she asked.

"Almost there," Randall said.

He turned on Halstead and saw the sign. Jutting out from the side of the building was a sign as tall as the building. The top said, 'David's', and stretching almost to ground level was the word, 'restaurant'. Ice cream, it announced below. Candies.

They walked past the big glass windows to the door on the corner. A bell jingled when the door closed. They found a booth and sat down across from each other, sitting in silence until a waitress came with two menus and two glasses of water. "Can I get you two anything else to drink?" she asked.

Randall read a name from the wall. "Royal Crown Cola, please. Two."

"On their way. I'll be back in a moment to take your order."

Once she had gone Randall pulled a handful of wadded dollar bills out of his pocket. He straightened them and laid them on the table between them. "Seven dollars," he said. "I found them on my desk. What do you want to eat?"

"Nothing."

"OK. I'll order for you anyway."

The waitress returned with the two colas. "And what have you decided?" she asked Randall. He ran a finger down the menu.

"Hmmm. How about David's Burger Plate for me, with cheese? Chili side with salad for my friend. An extra portion of French fries. Oh! Do you have any apple pie?"

"Freshly baked today."

"I'll have a piece of that. A la mode. And ... a piece of German chocolate cake," Randall handed both menus back to the waitress.

"Coming right up," she said.

"It's so hard to spend money in this place," Randall said once she was gone. "That's like, just over three bucks."

"You seem to be enjoying yourself," June said.

"Why not? Right now? We're alone in a diner about to have lunch. Look at this place!" Randall said.

"She's going to get us hurt. Really hurt."

"No, she won't. She'll be broken, just like us. And she'll do what she's told and Miss Beil will tell us why we're here and give us our assignment."

"I don't trust her. What did she do with her hand? She put it right through Miss Beil's desk like it was made of nothing but foam." June looked at her finger, put it on the Micalite table top and pressed down. She gave up a moment later.

"How's your face?" Randall asked.

"It hurts."

"It looks a little better. Why did she hit you?" he asked.

June hesitated. She avoided Randall's eyes. "I didn't finish my test."

"What was it?" Randall asked. He knew he was prying too far.

"It was gross. I couldn't go through with it. I almost did. I know she'll make me finish when I wake up," she said.

"It couldn't be as bad as mine."

"It ... it's just gross." June looked at Randall. Then leaned forward and whispered. "She's making me sleep with some fat, sweaty politician. I nearly puked when he started to put his hands all over me. There is no way you can know what that feels like. And I ran away from him and that crappy hotel room."

The waitress interrupted with plates of food. Steam rose off the chili in front of June. "What kind of dressing would you like, dear?" she asked.

"Green Goddess," Randall said. "You'll like that one," he said to June.

The waitress looked at Randall, then at June and the red welt running down her cheek. "Are you OK, Sweetie?" she asked.

"Yes," June said. She touched her face gingerly. "Just a stupid accident."

"Well, enjoy your lunch, and let me know if you need anything else." She lowered her voice. "It doesn't look that bad, I'm sure it will fade soon."

"Mind your own business," June said once she walked away.

Randall was already eating his burger. He chewed a bite, then swallowed. "June," he said. "When you do what she tells you, she does things for you." He toyed with the dollar bills on the table.

"And when you dream, it's not always bad dreams," he said.

"What she's asking is disgusting."

"And it's only once. Do it, get it over with, and it's done. Over. She doesn't make you do any more tests. She just gives you assignments. In

places like this." He took a couple French fries and dipped them in her chili. "This is a great combination!" he said.

"You'll do it," he added.

June sat silently looking at her lunch. She picked up her spoon and dipped it into her chili. She took a taste, and then put her spoon back on the table. Randall's appetite was obviously bigger.

"I know I will," she said. "She won't leave me alone until I do."

"Don't look real obvious like, but see that guy across the street, acting like he's reading a newspaper?" he asked. "No hat on." He tilted his head slightly towards the window before cutting into his pie.

Nadia looked across the street. It was busy. Practically all the men wore hats, which made it easy for June to spot one without. June watched him check his pocket watch, fold his paper and walk off.

"What about him?" she asked.

"Nothin' probably," Randall said. "It pays to be careful. Even here."

"You ever seen him before?"

"No," Randall said after a moment. "No, I don't think so."

He balanced a scoop of ice cream on top of his pie and shoveled both into his mouth. He swallowed and smiled. "Hey, how about a movie? It'll cheer you up."

"A movie?"

"Yeah. They're, like, all comedies, even the ones trying to be serious. Let's just find a theatre and see whatever's playing. They're good places to close your eyes and try to wake up." Randall picked up a couple of dollars from the table and put them in his pocket.

"Come on, we should be leaving anyway." He stood smiling at the empty plates. "That was good! Nothing beats burger and pie."

10

"Nadia, wake up!"

Nadia's mother tried to comfort her by cradling her head. Nadia screamed louder and flailed her hands trying to free herself. Her mother let go and sat on the edge of the bed, rubbing her cheek. Nadia opened her eyes wide, unable to focus, unable to make sense of what she was seeing. Eventually her breathing slowed. She noticed the familiar room, her yellow comforter, pictures on the wall, artwork found and copied from magazines. Her stereo. Books. The picture of her father standing in its frame. She turned to face her mother.

"There she is," her mother said. "There's my girl."

Nadia began to cry, softly at first. Her mother got into bed and lay next to her, holding Nadia in her arms.

"You're home now," she said. "You're safe now."

Nadia lay still and her mother let the silence settle between them, waiting for Nadia to talk.

"She sent the other two away," Nadia said.

"I was in the room alone with her. She had a knife and she cut me. She ..." Nadia started to cry again. Her mother held her tighter.

"She grabbed my head and squeezed," Nadia said after her crying subsided. "It felt like my skull was going to explode."

"Is this the first time she has touched you?" her mother asked.

Nadia looked at her hand, undamaged and smooth. "Yeah," she said. "She pulled a real sharp knife out of that desk of hers and ran the blade across my palm. Then she squeezed my head between her hands and told me to wake up."

Nadia's mother smelled her daughter's hair, trying to make sense of what she was told.

"Do you still think it is real, what is happening to you?" she asked.

"Of course, I do. It feels realer than real. Every time I go to sleep it's like I'm waking up." Nadia stopped. "She said she wanted me to hurt someone. To cut them. That's my test, she said."

"She's asking you to hurt somebody?"

"That's what she said. I don't want to go back there, mom. I just want to take something, just black me out until the morning. Take me to a doctor and get me pills ..."

"You aren't going to any doctor. All they'll do is take you away. You gotta be real careful who you talk to, Nadia. You can't trust no body or no thing in this system." She didn't have to argue with her daughter. Nadia knew what happened to people once the medical system got hold of them. Any system, for that matter.

"I just want to take a pill to make it all go black," she said anyway.

"I know, honey. I know. We'll figure something out," her mother said.

"Tell me about your nan," Nadia said.

"My nan, your great nan, always said to believe your dreams. She wasn't talking about no future wants to be, or schemes or designs. She was talking about in here, in you, in your mind. She said she saw wonderful places in her dreams, and could do wonderful things."

"What did she tell you, mom," Nadia said, replaying a comforting routine.

"She would travel in her dreams. She would talk to folks long dead, visit places in better times. Oh, the stories she would tell! She was like a sailor who had seen the entire world, every port and distant island, only I never heard of her venturing farther than Minneapolis, when she was awake. The only real journey she took was when her pa moved them up from Georgia."

"She met you once, just after you were born," Nadia's mom added. "She called you Nadia even before I told her your name. She took you in her arms and across the room, and you two had a real serious conversation. I tried to listen in, but Nan talked so softly I couldn't hear a thing. And I couldn't understand you anyway the way you just gurgled and burped."

"Tell me about your dream," Nadia said. "The one with the tree."

"The tree," her mother said. "OK. I was in the parking lot. That was the first hint. That's when I realized. I asked myself, *what do I need a car for when I am in a dream?* That's all it took, that awareness, to know. I looked at my hands, like you did in that classroom. Works every time. If you can see your hands, you can become aware. Awake, in a dream. So I started looking around. I found a car and started to travel down a road. I looked out the window and saw the countryside passing by. The fields were green—springtime had really begun. Everything was so vivid, so alive. I saw rolling fields stretching to the horizon. The blue of the sky seemed to ..."

"It was a real place, wasn't it?" Nadia asked. "Not just in your head."

"Oh, it was real," her mother said. "Just like where you go is real. It was just a different place, or time, or world."

"There was a tree in one field, standing by itself," she continued, "an ash tree, I think. I am certain it was. I got out of the car and walked to it. Its branches were as wide as it was tall, and I could almost feel the roots underneath, spreading into the earth and mirroring those above.

I felt like that tree was speaking to me, that I was really meant to go to it, to sit under it. I don't know. But I didn't. I just carried on past. I was scared, I guess. Part of me thinks my nan was there, wanting to tell me something. It felt like more, though. It felt like the whole universe was there. But I passed it and kept going. I was too scared to stop.

"I remember feeling dissatisfied with everything around me for weeks after I woke, because nothing could quite measure up to that aliveness. Your dad called it postpartum depression. But I knew better. I really think it was the same aliveness Nan would see. But that was the only time I was able to go there. Even after years I can still see that tree, I can still feel it calling."

She felt her daughter relax in her arms. "We'll figure this out, Nadia," she said. She tried to remember everything her nan had ever told her about dreams.

"Don't let me fall asleep again," Nadia said.

"I won't," she answered. She knew that her daughter would have to sleep sometime. All she could do was hold her when she woke screaming, and worry about the dark rings forming under her eyes.

*N*adia opened her eyes and looked around the classroom. She thought it was empty until she saw Miss Beil sitting very still behind her large wooden desk. She was frowning at Nadia. Nadia met her gaze, then looked away. She studied the blank blackboard, moved her eyes along the windows. She glanced at the door to the outside world. Her eyes finally rested on her desktop, and her hands resting on top of it. She pressed her index finger and it began to sink into the wood. She lifted her finger until it was an inch above the surface, and she pressed it down again, burying her finger up to the first knuckle, then the second. Nadia removed it again and looked at her finger, first the top, studying the nail and the wrinkles of her knuckles, and then the underside. She looked up at Miss Beil. Neither of them smiled.

"I don't think you quite understand, Nadia," Miss Beil said. "When I give an assignment, I expect it to be completed."

Nadia lifted her finger, looking at it instead of Miss Beil, and she placed it back on the desktop. She began to press. She heard movement and before she could look up, Miss Beil was standing in front of her. Nadia raised her head and Miss Beil grasped it in her hands. Nadia felt helpless, felt the power in the other woman's grip. She sat still, at the mercy of the adult in front of her.

Nadia could feel Miss Beil's breath on her face. The pressure on her skull was increasing as Miss Beil's hands began to squeeze.

"There are consequences for not doing as you are told," Nadia heard Miss Beil say. She felt intense pain, and then her world went dark.

***

Nadia opened her eyes to a world of blinding white light. She opened her mouth to breathe and felt a fist slam into her chest as she inhaled cold air. She breathed in again, a gasp, and another fist punched her in the chest. She put her hands over her face, hands that felt like planks of wood. Her eyes hurt but she forced them open. The sky was a brutal, naked blue. It stretched from horizon to horizon. Wind cut through her, blowing dry snow. Her ankles burned. She looked down at her bare legs and the black leather shoes on her numbing feet. She bent over, trying to conserve heat, arms clasped around her chest, hands burying themselves under her arms, but finding no warmth.

She staggered forward. Around her stretched miles of frozen tundra. Snow drifted like sand in the wind, blurring any line between earth and sky, land and horizon. She turned her back to the wind, moved her leg forward and took a step. She couldn't feel her feet. She took another numb step, not daring to look down. A searing pain burned across her waist where the wind had found a gap in her dress. She took another step and stumbled, falling to the ground.

Nadia curled into a ball, the smallest shape she could make. Every breath hurt. Her nostril hairs froze. Her eyelashes fused together. She raised a hand to wipe them clear, but a numb stump merely hit her face. She reached down to push herself up, she watched a hand land in snow, watched herself push away to rise, but she couldn't feel anything except intense pain. Her entire body screamed as a thousand frozen needles stung any exposed surface. She moved a foot forward, a disembodied stump. She moved the other, losing all sensation in her leg. The world tilted and she fell. Her face slammed into the frozen ground.

She watched snow drift away, carried on an unceasing wind. She tried to rise, but her limbs wouldn't respond. Over the unrelenting howl of wind, she screamed at her limbs to move. Her body was a foreign object beyond her control. She tried to curl into an even smaller ball. She felt incredibly tired. Nadia looked at her legs and willed them to move, but they seemed disembodied. Not hers. She lay her head back onto the frozen ground and stared at the horizon. She surrendered to the pain, and the pain turned into a warmth, a calm. Nadia ceased to feel. She fixed her gaze on the ground in front of her. She watched frozen crystals blow past. She looked at a stone rubbed bare by the wind.

She felt helpless and exposed. She felt utterly alone. Nadia gasped for breath. Each inhalation felt like a stab in her throat. She tried to bring her hand to her face again, but her arms lay unresponsive beside her. She lay breathing into the snow, the dying warmth of her breath forming a small indentation beside her mouth.

She saw feet approach. She moved her eyes upward and saw a white dress whipped by the wind. The face of Miss Beil hovered over hers.

"I don't think you quite understand, Nadia," Miss Beil said. "When I give an assignment, I expect it to be completed."

And then she was alone again. The wind cut into her flesh. She shivered violently. Her ears were filled with the moan of the wind. The shivers subsided and she relaxed. She felt a warmth spread through her body.

***

Nadia shielded her eyes from the glare. The sun seemed to be closer, larger, brighter. She squinted and took in her surroundings. In every direction sand rolled away in large dunes. Wind blew the fine dust into patterns, ripples and waves, creating a haze on the horizon. She lowered her hands and looked at them. She saw her bare arms, the patterned dress, her black leather shoes. Sand was already filling them.

Nadia turned toward the sun. She closed her eyes and raised her face until the heat made her turn away. She began to walk, following the wind. Hot sand blew against her calves. Her prints were erased almost as fast as she made them. She slowly climbed the nearest dune, struggling through the thick sand. At the ridge of the dune she breathed in hot air, each breath burning her throat. She tried to swallow but there was no moisture in her mouth.

Around her she saw more dunes, sand stretching in every direction. In the valley of the dune beneath her she saw a dark shape and walked to it. Every step became painful. Her feet burned. The skin on her arms and her legs turned bright red. Her head ached. She stumbled as she descended the dune.

She reached the shape and fell to her knees. Sand bit into her raw flesh. She reached out and touched the leathery dry skin of the carcass in front of her. A long neck stretched away from the gangly body. A long leg bent at the knee. A rip in the hide exposed a gleaming white bone. Nadia tried to focus on the creature. She tried to make her mind form the word. She knew what it was, but couldn't identify it.

She looked around herself, at sand in every direction. She shook her head, trying to clear it, and she was seized by pain, as if her brain were trying to carve a way out of her skull. She retched and threw up on her legs. Her breathing became quick panting. She tried to rise but her legs didn't respond. She looked at the carcass of the animal in front of her.

"Camel," she croaked.

She felt her body bake in the heat. Her skin was dry. She stopped sweating as her body lost all moisture. Heat radiated from her skin. She could see it reddening, could feel it blistering. Her lips dried and cracked. Her head ached unbearably, as if a sharp spike tried to force its way out of her skull between her eyes. She felt nauseated. Her muscles spasmed and cramped, her heart began to race. The carcass faded in and out of focus.

The pain was worse than being utterly alone.

***

Nadia smelled the rich moist soil around her. She felt its coolness beneath her hand. She wiggled her fingers into the ground. She raised her hand to her nose. Her eyes slowly adjusted to the gloom and she saw that she was in a deep pit. Steep unclimbable walls surrounded her. Tree limbs reached above, illuminated by a full moon. She stood up and touched the wall. She walked around the pit, running her hand along the smooth surface. She looked up into the night.

"Hey!" she shouted. "Hey!"

The sounds of the jungle answered her. They increased in volume. The noise surrounded her like the walls of the pit. A movement caught her eye and she looked at her hand. A giant ant, half as long as her finger stood next to it on the wall. Its antennae twitched, its two front legs reached out and landed on her finger. It stepped onto her hand and slowly walked towards her wrist. Nadia stood still, staring down at the insect. Its large head seemed to swivel as it sensed her warmth.

Nadia breathed, and it struck. She screamed in agony, slapping her other hand on top of the ant, holding her damaged hand. She screamed again as another wave of pain followed the initial sting. Nadia stag-

gered back, as far as she could, mere steps, driving her back into the wall. She screamed again, grasping her hand tightly. Pain bored into her flesh, again and again.

Nadia slid to the ground, groaning. She rocked slightly, crying. Her hand shook and throbbed. She looked at where the ant had been on the wall and saw movement. Black shapes made their way down to the bottom of the pit and spread out along the floor, antennae waving. One came near, following its sense of smell. As it neared, Nadia flailed out with her foot, hitting it and burying it in the ground.

Others came toward her, silently and quickly. She kicked again, but one climbed onto her leg. A searing pain shot through her calf. She screamed. More ants climbed on her. Burning pain struck her arm. Her thigh exploded in agony. She jumped up, stumbling about the pit, but there was nowhere to go. She hit at herself. Her knee exploded. She fell to the ground, shaking and sobbing uncontrollably.

***

Nadia gasped for air. She clutched the edges of her desk to stop herself from shaking. It didn't work. Nadia watched as Miss Beil rose, walked around her large desk and stood in front of her. Only then did Nadia realize that there was no more pain.

Miss Beil put a hand on Nadia's head, working her fingers into Nadia's thick hair.

"I think you are starting to get it, my dear," Miss Beil said. "You wouldn't want to go there every night, now would you?"

Nadia stared at Miss Beil's dress, unable to respond.

Miss Beil's hand gripped Nadia's hair tightly, "no, Nadia. You wouldn't. Vicious little nasties all over you. Such pain! No. But you have some work to do. I suggest you wake up and do it."

12

Nadia slipped out of the house early and made her way to the L, the elevated train carrying Chicago's masses. She boarded the Red Line at 79th. She moved towards the back and took a seat. The doors closed and the train began to move, taking her into the city. Most of the other passengers sat in the rear with her. The train had come from the south side. The 'deep south'. It would take a few more miles before the front of the carriage started to fill with white passengers.

Nadia did a quick search on a school computer the day before. Jones was easy to find. He was a lawyer. He worked in the city. His firm took on hopeless cases. Harassment. Segregation suits. Safety Officer misconduct. Treading a fine line between civil rights and sedition. She was just going to check him out, she told herself, if only to try to placate Miss Beil. Nadia didn't know if Miss Beil was watching, or if she was still in a classroom in 1944. A small shiver ran down Nadia's back thinking about her.

The train lurched forward to the next station. "There's nowhere you can run to in a train," her mother told her. "You get into that tube and you're stuck." But she had to travel in the city, so her mother tried to teach her to be as safe as she could be. Don't use the overpass. "Criminals, rapists, whoever, they can follow you up the stairs on both sides, and whatcha you gonna do then?" Don't smartass at a checkpoint, just give them what they want. Whatever they want. Get home before curfew, or find a good place to hide. Always have your papers on you. Life lessons in the Windy City.

The dark faces around her helped her feel safer. She looked through the carriage door and into the car in front. A Metra was in the isle, hand on holster. The passenger he was looking down at was showing his papers. The train stopped again and the Metra and passenger got off together. Nadia opened her bag and checked for her own documents.

At Garfield the first white boarded. His long blond hair was out of place. But this was a University stop. Hipster, Nadia judged. He walked past the empty seats in the front of the carriage and continued down the aisle, taking a place across from Nadia. She glanced out of the corner of her eye to see him smiling, staring forward. Nadia looked out her window at the traffic streaming into town. When she turned again, he was looking at her.

"It's like a dream, this city," he said.

Nadia stared at him, suddenly alert.

"I mean, you look out the window and see all those sky ... sky-scrapers," he said. He looked out the window. The train was suddenly engulfed in dark as the line went underground.

"But then it's all gone," he said over the noise. "And we're plunged into dark tunnels, like some sort of nightmare."

The train pulled into Roosevelt and the doors opened. People filled the carriage. The doors closed again and the train moved off.

"Hey, sorry," the young man said. "Crazy person talking on the train. You going into the city?" he asked.

Nadia continued to stare forward, *"you get into that tube and you're stuck,"* her mother warned.

"I'm Jakob," he said.

Nadia continued to ignore the young man beside her.

"Here's my stop," he said standing. "Have a good morning!" He staggered up the aisle as the train came to a halt. When the doors opened, he quickly jumped out, avoiding another crush of commuters as they boarded. Nadia lost sight of him as the train moved forward.

At Chicago Street she left the train and rode the escalator to the surface. She felt dwarfed by the tall buildings, but secure in the anonymity of the crowded sidewalk. Moody students were out in force, handing out leaflets to the morning rush.

"Thank you, sister," Nadia said as she took one. She walked past the campus and up another block, stopping in front of a tall brown stone building. She moved away from the entrance, towards a coffee shop in the front of the building. She leaned against the wall and pretended to read the leaflet. On the glossy cover was an American flag and a cross. "God loves America!" it proclaimed, "and Jesus loves you!" it told Nadia. She looked at the bearded white man with outstretched arms on the paper.

Nadia watched the people in the coffee shop. That is where he might be, starting each day with a paper cup in his hand. Everybody seemed to be holding one, a paper cup with a plastic lid, some sort of urban fashion accessory. She scanned the faces, mostly white. Then she saw him. He smiled at the cashier as he took his drink. He carried a briefcase in his other hand. Nadia watched him thank a woman for holding the door open, and he stepped into the street.

He was more handsome than Miss Beil described. He looked more athlete than lawyer. His grey suit didn't hide the strong shoulders underneath. He turned and Nadia watched him walk into a tall building. Her eyes moved the length of his body. She shook her head and looked at her watch, wondering if she still had time to get back to school before the first bell.

13

13

*M*iss Beil stood and walked over to June. She rested a hand on the girl's blonde hair before running her fingers through it. She stroked her head one more time. She stroked June's face with the back of her hand, savoring the smooth feel of the girl's face.

"My dear June," she said, "my sweet, sweet, June."

Miss Beil rested her hand on June's head. Her hand slipped to the back of the girl's neck where it stopped. She leaned over, inhaling the scent of her hair. "Well done," she whispered.

June sat absolutely still. Tears formed in her eyes, spilling over and running down her cheeks. Miss Beil turned and looked at Nadia and Randall. She walked slowly to her desk, opened the drawer and removed a glass jar.

"This is today's lesson, class," she said. She lifted the jar to her eyes, studying the insect within. It was long and black. Its front legs pawed at the smooth glass, unable to find traction and climb to the lid. Its antennae waved frantically. Miss Beil smiled.

"This, class, is what is known as the bullet ant," she said, holding up the jar. "Or paraponera clavata, to use its proper name. It is from Latin America. The word ponera is actually from the Greek, ponira, which means wretched or wicked. Such a beautiful word. It is said that the sting *of the bullet ant hurts just like a bullet ripping through your flesh. Only, I am told, the pain doesn't end as fast. It keeps banging away for hours."*

Miss Beil looked at Nadia and smiled. "It lives in colonies and harvests nectar, just like a honey bee. If it stings, it's because it feels threatened. It is very protective of its hive." Miss Beil slowly unscrewed the lid of the jar. "Such an admirable trait, don't you think? It will do anything to defend the colony, even sacrifice itself.

"But before it does that, it will inflict incredible pain on its enemy." Miss Beil was still looking at Nadia. Nadia shifted in her seat. She could see June and Randall sitting stock still, eyes forward. "The pain acts as a deterrent. Once stung, its enemy knows it should stay away.

"The natives of the Brazilian rainforest have a rite of passage that involves our friend here," Miss Beil continued. "To become a warrior a youth is required to put his hand into a glove woven from leaves. The glove, of course, is full of paraponera clavata, and the would-be warrior must keep his, or her, in this case, hand in the glove for a full five minutes."

"Imagine that, Nadia," she said. "But here is the truly interesting part. The young warriors do not do this one time only. They go through it again and again over a period of months. Day after day, night after night. Night. After. Night."

Miss Beil stepped forward, walking slowly until she was in front of Nadia's desk. Nadia's eyes didn't leave the jar containing the ant. "Imagine that, Nadia. Night after night, until they prove themselves worthy."

"Put out your hand, Nadia," Miss Beil asked.

Nadia didn't move. Her hands gripped the sides of her desk.

"Come now, Nadia. We have important lessons to learn. That is why we are in school."

Nadia looked at Miss Beil, into her cold green eyes. Miss Beil continued to smile. "Randall, can you help Nadia in today's lesson, please?"

Randall shifted in his desk. "Come along, boy," she said firmly.

He rose and walked over to Nadia. "Her hand, please."

Randall reach down and grabbed Nadia's wrist. He looked quickly at her and mouthed the words, "I'm sorry." He pulled her hand free and held it on the surface of the desk. Nadia looked fearfully, first at Randall, then at Miss Beil. She watched wide eyed as Miss Beil brought the jar closer, turning it over onto the back of Nadia's hand. The ant fell, landing on her flesh. Its antennae waved frantically. Then it raised its abdomen and lowered it.

Nadia screamed. She tried to rise but was trapped at her desk. Randall continued to hold her arm firmly. The muscles in her arm spasmed. Another wave of pain exploded in her hand. The ant's abdomen rose again and injected another dose of venom. Nadia continued to scream.

Miss Beil lifted the jar and removed the ant. She walked back to her desk, put the lid on the jar and placed the jar in her desk drawer. She closed the drawer and sat down. Randall let go of Nadia's arm and returned to his desk. Nadia cradled her hand and rocked back and forth moaning. Waves of pain struck her. The others sat silently watching her.

"Nadia," Miss Beil said, "I don't know if you can hear me now, but I think you know what I am saying. We are in school to learn our lessons. The sooner we learn, the sooner we can progress."

"Well," Miss Beil finally said. "Enough for today class. I suppose I will see you tomorrow night, Nadia."

Nadia didn't notice the others leave the room. She continued to cradle her hand and rock.

14

Nadia woke up slapping at her hand. Her mother tried to hold her, but Nadia pushed away. She stumbled out of bed and put her hands on her knees, catching her breath. Her heart slowly stopped racing. Her mother gently put her arm around Nadia. They both had dark rings under their eyes from night after night of disturbed sleep.

"Nadia, is there anything I can do?" she asked.

Nadia stood up straight and shook her head. "No, mom, I'll be OK," she said. "Just go back to bed. I'll sit out here for a while."

Nadia left her room and walked to the lounge. She sat on the faded green sofa and waited for her mother to go back to her bed. Light from the early dawn was beginning to filter through the windows. Nadia got up and walked to the wooden rocking chair, sat down and rocked back and forth. The motion soothed her. She looked at her hands grasping the armrests. She willed them to relax, but they wouldn't let go.

Restless, she got up again and went into the kitchen. She reached the counter and slowly opened the second drawer. She reached in and picked up what she knew was there, a knife with a blade the length of her hand. She gripped the handle tightly, testing the grip.

Nadia walked silently to the front door where her bag lay. She opened it, and placed the knife along the bottom. She closed the bag and returned to the rocking chair. As the room lightened Nadia went to her room and dressed. She went to her mother's room where she lay in an exhausted sleep. Nadia bent and kissed her. Her mother opened her eyes and smiled.

"I'm going to school early, mom," Nadia said.

"OK, honey," her mother answered. She slowly closed her eyes and quickly fell back to sleep.

Nadia checked the street before stepping out. It was deserted. She walked to the end and turned into the alley behind the houses. She might wake a dog or two, but she wouldn't see any S-O. They tended to avoid potential ambushes. These were the streets behind the streets, the world of the people. She carefully checked each crossing and ran across to the next alley.

At 79th street she had no choice but to walk along the sidewalk. She was just a student on her way to school. She walked past boarded up store fronts. Closed liquor stores. Posters of straight- haired women offered the way to *real* beauty. She waited at a stop until a bus arrived, paid, boarded and sat as close to the doors as she could.

She disembarked and entered the L station, swiping her card at the turnstile. She looked at her card, realizing too late that it could easily be traced. She walked to the platform letting the sound of the expressway empty her mind. When the next train arrived, she entered and took a seat in the rear. She took her papers out of her bag and stuck them in the front pocket of her jeans with her card.

She knew the way from the Chicago Street station. She walked quickly to the brownstone building knowing she would be early. She leaned against the wall of a building, dwarfed in the concrete canyon, lost among the morning crowd. Her hand went into her bag, pushing its way to the bottom. She found the handle and gripped it. She saw Jones enter the coffee shop and took a slow step towards the door. She watched him pay, smile at the cashier, pick up his briefcase. He turned his back to the door and pushed it open. When he turned around Nadia was standing in front of him.

Nadia pulled her hand from her bag, swung widely and felt a hard shove. She staggered and fell to the ground. The wind was knocked out of her as a weight fell on top of her.

"Get up and run," a voice growled in her ear.

She felt herself being dragged to her feet. Her bag fell and emptied on the road. The knife clattered into the gutter. A strong hand pulled her down the sidewalk. She tried to free her wrist but followed along, just managing to stay upright. She lurched around a corner and looked at the arm she was attached to. It was white. She glanced up and saw long blond hair, then quickly focused on the ground and staying on her feet.

Cars honked as she was pulled across the street. They ran to the end of the block and ducked around the corner. The young man pushed her up against the wall and looked quickly to the left and right.

"Just follow me. We need to talk," he told her. "Catch your breath and try to look normal."

She followed as he walked along the side of the building. At the back of the building they crossed another street. They hurried down a block and turned towards the metro station ahead. She followed him up the stairs to the station. When he reached the turnstiles, he stopped. Nadia reached into her pocket and pulled out her card. She waved it twice over the monitor and they both rushed to a southbound train. They jumped on as the doors were closing and walked to the rear of the carriage.

Nadia looked at the young man sitting next to her. He stared forward, breathing heavily.

"I know you," she said. "I saw you before. Are you following me?"

He turned towards her. "Yes, I am. Which is lucky for you," he said. "We met on the train. I'm Jakob."

"Lucky?" she started, but stopped as he raised a finger to his lips. He raised his eyebrows and indicated to the passengers sitting nearby. He shook his head slightly and faced forwarded again

as the train moved south.

Nadia shifted uncomfortably next to him. She glanced down and realized for the first time that she did not have her bag. She tried to remember what was in it, but was certain there was enough to identify her. Part of her relaxed. She didn't care. She did what Miss Beil wanted. She would get to sleep tonight.

15

They got out of the train in Englewood. She continued to walk behind him until she was certain he didn't know where he was going.

"Follow me," she said as she brushed past him. She saw a sign and walked towards it. Jamaican Jerk Chicken. A green, black and yellow flag was by the door. It looked like it might be a safe place, somewhere S-O usually didn't eat. Nadia opened the door and entered the dark eatery.

A dark man with long dreadlocks looked at her, and then at the blond-haired man behind her.

"I think you have the wrong place," he said.

"Please," Nadia said. She pleaded with her eyes. "We just need a place to ..." Nadia glanced back the door leading to the street.

"Fine," he said after a pause. "Sit at the back." He watched silently as they walked past him and took a booth at the rear of the restaurant. They sat unmoving until he walked to them.

"I'd give you a menu but you know what's on it," he said.

Nadia looked across the table. "Do you have any money?" she asked.

"Yes."

Nadia nodded to the dark man and he disappeared into the kitchen.

"Who are you?" she asked when they were alone.

"My name is Jakob Iverson," he answered.

"Why are you following me?" Nadia asked.

"To stop you from doing something stupid," he said.

"Looks like you failed," Nadia said.

Her lips quivered as her eyes filled with tears. She tried to hold back the torrent but couldn't. She sobbed loudly. The man came out of the kitchen and looked at the two, the tall long-haired white boy and the sobbing black girl across from him. He reached down and grabbed Jakob roughly by his shirt and raised him out of his seat.

"What did you do to that girl!" he demanded. "You leave her be and get the hell out of here!" He started to drag Jakob away from the table.

"No! Don't," Nadia pleaded. She jumped up and put a hand on his arm. "He helped me, he didn't hurt me!"

"Helped?"

"Yeah, he helped me, and now we have to figure out what to do next," she said.

The three stood looking at each other for a moment. Finally, the man let go of Jakob's shirt. He turned to Nadia, studied her face and looked into her eyes.

"We need a place for a while," she said. Her hand was still resting on his arm.

"OK," he said. "Just call me if you need anything. My name is Frank."

"Thank you," Nadia said. She sat back at the table.

Jakob straightened his shirt as Frank walked back to the kitchen.

"Listen, you didn't kill him. You didn't even hurt him. All you did was probably ruin an expensive suit," Jakob said.

An expression of relief passed briefly across her face, followed by a type of fear she didn't allow herself to feel on the train. She had attacked a man with a knife and she wasn't going to get away with that.

"Why did she want you to do that?" he asked.

Nadia stared across the table, mouth open. "How do you know about her?" she finally managed.

"I don't know about her. I just know about her kind," he said.

"What does that mean?" Nadia asked. Frank came out of the kitchen with two plates of food. He set them down slowly and went back into the kitchen.

"Well?" she asked.

Jakob looked at the food in front of him. He picked up a chicken wing and smelled it. He smiled and took a bite.

"I dream," he said, "like you. Dreams where you're somewhere else, or somewhen else. And that are somehow *very* real."

Jakob took a bite, relishing the meat.

16

"Everybody dreams," Jakob began, "but not everybody knows why or even remembers them. I mean, there are a lot of things dreams do. They help the mind process the day's events, they help cleanse the subconscious or whatever you want to call it. But you know I'm not talking about those types of dreams."

Nadia sat back, listening. Her food remained untouched.

"The dreams you have are beyond vivid. You don't just see, you feel. You interact with others. They are not part of your own mind. They're dreams you don't want to tell anybody about because they would think you were crazy. Imagine losing touch of what is real and what is a dream, when everything you dream is, in truth, real.

She wanted Jakob to keep talking. It helped keep her mind off what she did and what might happen to her, at least for the moment.

"These dreams are called lucid. But they are more than that. Because they are real. And when we dream like that, we become a magnet to something that sees us as a tool. In my first dream I wandered around an ancient city, finally finding a temple, a magnificent temple. It had a forest of marble columns, adorned with statues of Valkyries and chariots. I didn't know what was happening. I just thought it was an incredibly intense dream. But for weeks after I could feel her."

"Her?" Nadia asked. "Miss Beil?"

"Not Miss Beil. The goddess that brought me. She wanted, or needed, me to do something. It is what they do. She called me back, and I would dream, until I did what she wanted. I didn't understand that I didn't have to, not in the beginning. Her name was Artemis. Some call her Diana."

"Are you saying Miss Beil is a goddess?" Nadia whispered.

"The words 'goddess' or 'god' aren't the best ones to use. Those are confusing terms. We think of gods as some sort of higher beings, all powerful, all knowing. But there's no such thing. The gods exist because we do. They need us. To do the things they can't. Remember that."

Nadia looked around. The restaurant was filling, but the other customers sat closer to the entrance.

"How do you know this?" she asked.

"I've been dreaming this way for years," he said. "At first, I felt helpless, and maybe I was because I didn't understand it enough. I was used, that's for sure. Artemis, I don't know, saw my potential, that I was awake in my dreams, and she used me to do something. She said it was to protect my reality—"

"Your *reality*?"

"My time and place. Where I'm from. It's a lot different than here."

"You're saying you're from a different reality?"

"That's exactly what I'm saying." Jakob took a bite of his meal. "There's lots of realities. Lots of time lines. I didn't know that when I first met Artemis, that's why I did what she asked."

"And what was that?" Nadia asked.

Jakob pushed the remains of his meal away. "To kill somebody," he said. "When I dreamed, I was in my past, just like you are in your past when you dream. I had to ..." Jakob looked at his hands, remembering the knife covered in blood, the dead man beneath him. "She showed me realities where he didn't die, where he was called 'The Great', and where my people were not." Jakob used the back of a knuckle to wipe his eye.

"They're like humans in some ways," he said. "They live and die, it just takes a much, much longer time. Can you name the gods of the ancient Assyrians?"

"I don't even know who the ancient Assyrians were," Nadia answered.

"Exactly. The Assyrians were an ancient people, probably the earliest thing we call civilization, based in Mesopotamia or around there. They had a god, or more likely more than one, but the Assyrians eventually faded away. And so did their gods. Even the Neanderthals had gods, but when they ceased to exist, their gods went with them. Maybe some held on and survived a bit longer in another form. A god of wind, or a god of fire, whatever. No doubt those who did last longer used dreamers to help them. The temple I stood before was made to worship Artemis. Have you ever heard of her? The Romans called her Diana. My people call her *Skade*. She had names even before that. She was called Ceres before the Greeks or the Romans gave her a name. She is not the only one. There are a host of gods and goddess trying to survive, trying to shape ..."

Jakob stopped talking and concentrated on his food. Nadia looked at him without expression. He finished his chicken and wiped his hands on a napkin.

"Look. The thing is, they can't do it themselves. They're just energy, really. They want to shape reality to their liking. That's why they need us. Try to imagine a tree that holds everything. It holds every world, every reality. A world tree."

"My mom told me about a tree, a dream about a tree, that seemed to hold many worlds," Nadia said.

"A tree is a good analogy. My culture describes a tree of many worlds and realities—"

"What culture is that?"

"Norse culture. I forget that you're brought up with different stories. The people of the north. The Danelaw."

Nadia looked at Jakob. He could see her doubt.

"You've heard of Vikings?" he asked.

"Of course," she said. "You're telling me you're a Viking?"

"I'm a Norseman," he said. "In my reality I live in a city called London."

"The capital of England?"

"No, Yorvik is the capital. You see? It's a different reality, a whole different world. Maybe it's different because of what I did. There are times when a reality can branch out. Like a new limb growing on a tree. Something is changed. Maybe a person dies—"

"Miss Beil talked about assassinations, and babies being killed," Nadia interrupted.

"She sounds charming," Jakob said. "But sometimes one person dying can change or create a new reality. They are pivotal people, in pivotal moments. That's why those moments are so important."

Jakob stopped so Nadia could take in some of what he was saying. He knew much of it would take a lot of time to process.

"Nadia, I learned that dreaming does not have to be controlled by them," Jakob continued. "We can learn to control our dreams. That's partly why I am here, or how I'm here. Miss Cassy Beil has a hold over you—"

"A hold?" Nadia asked. "She has more than that. You don't know what she does."

"No, I don't. But I can see it's bad," Jakob admitted. "There is a way to change that. We just need to learn more. And we need to figure out what she wants. Has she told you what she wants?"

"She said she wants a President elected."

"Who could be a pivotal person at a pivotal moment," Jakob said.

"And she gives us 'tests' to complete. Things we had to do," Nadia said.

"Like today?"

Nadia scowled. "Yes," she said. "She calls it training."

"For what she wants you do in 1944."

"Is your world as messed up as this one?" she asked.

"It's different," he admitted. "In my world, this place doesn't exist, which probably means it's not as messed up, as you say. The lake and the forests and the rivers are there, of course. But not this city. There are other cities along the shore, smaller cities that are all part of the Greater League."

"What is that?" Nadia asked.

"The tribal alliance. What started as the Iroquois League, and grew as more tribes joined. It is the most powerful nation on this continent, stretching all the way to the Mississippi. Our settlements on the eastern seaboard exist because they let us. We're like their middle man in dealing with the Islamic Republics of Europa and the Afrika Kingdoms."

"You're confusing me," Nadia shook her head.

"When you become more in control of your dreams, you can see," he said.

Jakob pulled a bill out of his pocket. He smoothed it out on the table top and turned it over. "Look at this," he said. "Can you read that?"

"In God we trust," she said.

"Well, don't. Don't ever do that. Where there are many, they keep a sort of balance. They play their games and play with us, just like you read about in mythology. They whisper in your ear or use you in a dream. But where there are fewer, or even just one ... it is very dangerous. Like in this reality. I've seen a reality where there are bombs that can destroy entire cities, and that have even been used. Great wars fought between nations, world wars, like in your 1944. Each of those realities was dominated by a single god. *Gott mit uns!* Soldiers actually wore that on their clothing . It's from a Germanic language—it means, God is with us! Or they shout *Allahu akbar!* God is Great! A god is never with us, and a god is never great."

"We have bombs that destroy cities," Nadia said. "They're called nuclear bombs."

"And you have one god." Jakob pointed to the dollar. "It says so, right here."

"For now," he said. "Just play along until we know what's happening."

Nadia looked at Jakob with confusion. Before she could ask for meaning Frank walked to the table and indicated to the window. The sun had set and the sky was darkening. The last customer had already left.

"It's near curfew," he said. "I can take you to your place if isn't too far. But we better leave now. This guy might get off with a warning, but I don't think we'd be so fortunate. Where do you live?"

"Gresham," Nadia answered.

"Come on then. What about you? You don't look like a local," he said to Jakob.

"You could just let me out in an alley," he said.

"That'll be easy, because that'll be our main route. Only scrappers hunting their metal at this time of the evening."

Frank drove with his lights off despite the increasing dark. He crossed each street only after checking both directions. Except for feral cats, the alleys were empty. Jakob asked him stop behind a large garage and got out of the car. He leaned through Nadia's window and said into her ear, "hang in there. Do as she says. Things are probably going to get very rough, but stay strong. We'll figure this out. I'll see you again," and then he walked away into the shadows.

"Ain't even gonna ask," Frank said. He drove carefully and stopped the car on the corner of Nadia's street. She could see her house. The street was empty.

"OK trouble," he said. "Just get out and go. Be careful."

Nadia slipped out of the car, closing the door silently. She ran down the walk, up the broken stairs to her front door, and disappeared inside.

17

“**N**adia, wake up!”

Nadia’s mother sounded frantic. She shook her daughter roughly. Nadia heard a pounding on the door. She heard a shout.

“Police! Stay where you are! Police! Stay where you are!”

Nadia’s mother ran into the front room as the door splintered and fell open. Armed men in black stormed in. The butt of a rifle flashed through the air and hurled her to the ground. A man stood over her, pointing his assault rifle at her.

Shouts filled the room as men kicked open doors. Strong hands roughly grabbed Nadia's hair and lifted her from bed. An S-O threw her to the floor and knelt on the center of her back with his full weight. He drove his knee pad down hard, grabbed her hands and bent them behind her back. Her bound them with a sharp plastic tie before grabbed another handful of hair and dragging her into the front room.

She saw black boots out of the corner of her eye. Her mother lay in front, blood smearing her cheek. Her mother looked at her, mouth clenched tight, wearing an expression of pure hatred. Sounds of crashing filled the house as drawers were flung to the ground, cupboards emptied. Glass shattered as it was cleared off a countertop. Finally, the noise stopped.

"Clear!"

An officer pulled Nadia's head back and looked at her face before shoving it back onto the floor.

"Bring the girl," he ordered.

The officer kneeling on Nadia jerked her to her feet, arms stretched painfully behind her. She looked over at the wreckage of the room. Another officer stood pointing his rifle at her still prone mother. Like the others, he too wore a balaclava. As Nadia was dragged to the front door, her mother tried to rise but the S-O standing over her put a heavy boot onto her back and stood with it there. He pulled the action back on his rifle.

"Stand down, mama," he said.

"Nadia Ifedi?" an officer asked.

Nadia looked at him, stunned and confused. He slapped her face.

"Nadia Ifedi?" he asked again.

Nadia tasted blood. She nodded. He slapped her again.

"Are you Nadia Ifedi?" he asked. "Speak up!"

"Yes," she gasped.

"Get her to the station," he said to the man holding Nadia.

The S-O turned Nadia around and faced the night. Blue and red flashing lights lit the street. He pushed her towards one of the black SUVs blocking the street with Chicago Police painted in white on the side. He opened a door, bent her head sharply down, and shoved her into the back seat, slamming the door. Two officers got in front and the vehicle began to move.

Dark streets passed as they drove, the men in front silent. Stopping in front of a brick building with tall glass doors, an S-O dragged her out of the back seat and marched her through the doors. He pushed Nadia past the front desk, down a tiled corridor and into a small room with a metal table fixed to the floor. He shoved her into a chair and put a cuff around one of her wrists, the other cuff to a table leg. He cut the plastic tie around her hands and left the room, slamming the door behind him.

Nadia lost track of time. A draft from a vent high on the wall blew down on her and she shivered. With her free hand she rubbed her bare legs. All she wore was what she was sleeping in. She pulled her t-shirt over her panties and squeezed her knees together, rocking slightly trying to keep cold and terror at bay.

Finally, the door opened and a uniformed officer came in. He sat down in front of her. He showed her the knife she had taken from home.

"Nadia Ifedi. Is this your knife?" he asked.

"Yes," she said. They were the first words she had spoken since leaving her house.

"You are in a great deal of trouble. You probably won't leave this place. Not until we find out who you are with and root out the entire cell. Even then I doubt you'll leave. There's enough NLM scum on the street already. Are you in the Negro Liberation Movement, Nadia? Honesty will save us both a lot of time and trouble."

"No!" Nadia said.

"Who are you working with? Is your mother involved?" he asked.

"No!" Nadia said again, louder.

His hand flew across the table, connecting with her face. Nadia cried out in pain.

"Is your mother NLM like you? You can tell me," he said.

"No! She isn't! I'm not!"

He hit her again. "We can do this all night until you confess. Who are you working with? Your metro card was swiped twice after the assault. Who were you working with?"

"Nobody!"

He slapped her again. Nadia began to sob. "Who, Nadia? Who are you working with?"

"Nobody!" she pleaded. He raised his hand and Nadia flinched. "She made me do it!" Nadia cried.

"Who, Nadia, Your mother?"

"No! No! *She* made me do it, not my mom! *She* made me!" Nadia said.

"Who is she, Nadia?"

"The woman in my dreams!"

"The what?" he asked.

"In my dreams! She hurts me, she hurts me until I do what she says!" Nadia said.

This time the officer didn't hold back. The sound of a slap echoed off the walls. Nadia cried out loudly.

"Don't fuck with me nigger, give me some names!" he growled.

Nadia couldn't stop crying. She shrunk away from the officer. "She hurts me," Nadia said, over and over. "She hurts me."

The officer stood and looked at the girl across the table, rocking backward and forward, eyes looking past him, continuing to say it over and over again. "She hurts me, she hurts me."

He walked to the door and opened it.

"Psych!" he shouted.

When Nadia's mother was allowed to collect her one week later, Nadia looked at her but showed no recognition. Her mouth hung open. Saliva ran down her chin. Her face was bruised. Her temples showed burns from the electroshock treatment. A psychologist handed her mother bottles of medication and gave instructions in a bored monotone. An S-O handed her a court order with more instructions. Her mother took each, seeing them for the shackles they represented.

She signed papers. Then she was allowed to take her broken daughter back to their broken house, to slowly put both back together.

18

*M*iss Beil sat at her desk with her hands folded in front of her. She looked at her students and smiled. June, Randall, and Nadia kept their eyes on their desks. Their hands were in their laps. They were completely silent and completely still. Her smile grew. She was satisfied. She rose from her seat and walked to where they sat. She walked beside each of them, and as she passed noted not a single glance, a single movement.

"My warriors," she said. "You have done very well. I am so proud of you. We've had some time off from class, a short time, but I'm sure you used it well, to rest up and be ready."

She walked to where June was sitting, reached out slowly and stroked the girl's hair. June stiffened under her touch, but only Miss Beil noticed.

"My dear June. You were such a brave girl. Sometimes we have to do things we don't like. It's just part of our lot. You're learning what it means to be a woman," she said. She continued to slowly stroke the girl's hair until she slid her hand down to June's neck and leaned close to her ear.

"Well done," she said.

Miss Beil stepped between the desks until she stood next to Nadia. Nadia kept completely still. She held her breath. If it were possible, she *would have stopped her heart beating. Miss Beil reached down and put a hand on Nadia's shoulder. Nadia exhaled slowly.*

"Nadia. Nadia. Nadia," Miss Beil said. "You went through the wars and you are a warrior. Warriors do what must be done, because there is nobody else to do it. Your strength has impressed me. Yes, it truly has. Look at me, Nadia."

Nadia slowly turned her head until her eyes met Miss Beil's. "You see, I am proud of you," she said, bending closer. "Remember that the mind is its own place, and in itself can make a heaven of hell, or a hell of heaven." Miss Beil released Nadia's shoulder and stood up straight.

"I am proud of all of you. Today we are ready to begin," Miss Beil said as she walked to her desk. She perched on the top of its wooden surface. "Look this way, please."

"Long ago," Miss Beil said, "There was a time of peace. There was balance. The angels reigned over creation as equals. But like any time of peace it was based on lies. One angel was raised above the others, made the heir to all creation, called the 'Son'. And the balance was shattered. The others were told to bow before Him. Imagine that! For many of us, it was too humiliating."

Her three students sat watching her.

"So," she continued, "there was a terrible war, one that laid the ground for all the wars to follow, even that little show going on out there." Miss Beil gestured towards the windows, a flick of her wrist.

"Like in all wars there were heroes. Maybe I should call you that," she said. "My heroes. Yes. I will do that," she smiled at the three.

"Like all wars," she said, "there were heroes, and the rebel commander, our hero, was magnificent. It was he that rallied the many, he that cried for justice. He needed only open his mouth and speak, and all ears bent to listen. Leaders try to pass on their mantel to their sons, and their nepotism always becomes despotism—this he knew quite clearly. 'Here at

last we shall be free,' he cried, and we came to his side. Our leader stood gallantly against that. He stood gallantly for equality, for fraternity, for democracy. To see him that day! Nothing could exceed his energy and character. He did not shy from his Promethean task. Nor did his Heroes. He faced his enemy, clad in armor of gold, spear and shield in hand. 'Follow me!' he cried. Future poets would sing of their glory:

> Ten thousand banners rise into the air
> With orient colors waving: with them rose
> A forest huge of spears: and thronging helms
> Appeared, and serried shields in thick array
> Of depth immeasurable: anon they move.

"I love that part," Miss Beil said, "but outnumbered they fell. They fell back, they gave up their sacred ground. Yet they were not beaten."

Miss Beil looked at her three students, "you've obviously not read your Milton like good little school children. Paradise Lost? No? Probably not even Dante. His Inferno is my favorite. Such vivid descriptions of home."

Their mouths were slightly open as they stared at her.

"The leader led his people away from the field of battle and into exile. Like Aeneas after the fall of Troy, who took his people across the Aegean and founded a new city on a hill, a shining beacon, an empire spanning the known world. All from the seeds of defeat. The great leader of whom I speak did just that. Only his empire did not fade into history, it did not leave magnificent ruins. No, this leader never gave up or faded away. The battlefield may have changed, but the battle remains the same. He and his people will never bow down. We will continue to pay any price. We will continue to be our own masters until the final battle. That is what we are preparing for, that is what we have a part to play in.

"You may not understand what I am saying right now. But you will," she said. *"Everything you do, from now on, has a role to play. So, pay attention, and be alert. There is so much to do."*

"But not today. Today I want you to go out and enjoy the city. You earned it. I want you to explore. Look at the buildings. Such fine architecture. There is a very interesting complex. It's boxy, but it's beautiful. It has the cutest name," she said.

The three students sat at their desks. "Off you go, now," she said. *"Have yourselves some fun." Miss Beil waved towards the door. Each got up and walked towards the exit.*

"And children," she said as they were leaving, *"Previously, we have been quite formal in class, as we had to be. But from now on I want to change that, as we will be working together. So please, call me Cassy."*

19

"Calling her Cassy don't change who she is," Nadia said when they were on the street.

June glanced at Nadia. "She'll still hurt you," Nadia added.

"I don't think it will be like that anymore," Randall said. "Hey," he added, "I'm sorry about that arm thing."

"Just doin' what you're told," Nadia said.

"No, really," he said.

"OK. Whatever. Where are we going anyway?" she asked.

"To look at a 'boxy, but beautiful' building, didn't you hear her?" he said. "That's why we're out here. I'm pretty sure it's that one over there." They walked down the crowded street, away from the city center. Nadia heard the popping of electric sparks and watched a bus follow the cables suspended above the street.

They walked in silence for a block. Then Randall stopped and pointed down the street to a large rectangular stone building. Long narrow windows ran down the sides of the walls. Red, white and blue flags adorned the top of the building. It looked like a factory. A long sign ran nearly the height of the building. Randall read it out loud.

"Stadium. It's the old sports stadium, where the Blackhawks played!" he said. "Wow!" He looked at June and Nadia, who weren't showing the

appropriate amount of enthusiasm. "The Blackhawks! Ice hockey, you know? Geez, girls! It'd be great to see a game!"

"Listen to him, he's having the time of his life," Nadia said to June. "I don't think a sports game is going on."

Flags and banners were being erected in front of the grey building, adding a patriotic air. Men in suits and women in dresses walked past workmen in denim. June, Nadia, and Randall stepped into the crowd and walked closer to the stadium. Nadia studied the faces of those passing, becoming more and more alive to what she was seeing.

"That was President Wallace!" Nadia said to the two. They both stopped and turned around, at the same time a small group of men turned. The tallest amongst them tilted his head and considered the three. He stepped towards them, looking down, a full head above. Despite his shirt and tie, his smile expressed an amicable nature.

"What was that you called me, young lady?" the tall man asked Nadia.

"Sorry, sir," she said. "I meant vice president."

"Don't be sorry," he said. "I heard you say, 'Mr. President.' I'll take that as an omen for how things might work out this week." He smiled. "Mr. President," he said to the men next to him. They laughed.

"You will make a fine President, sir," Nadia said.

"If I am called to the job, I hope I can live up to your expectations," he said. "What is your name?" he asked.

"Nadia, sir," she answered.

"Please, 'Mr. President' will do," he said, eliciting more laughs from his companions.

"And your friends?" he asked.

"June, sir," June said.

"Randall, sir."

He shook their hands, smiling warmly at each as he did. "Well, we have a great deal of work to do," he said, "and we best get on to it." He reached into a pocket and took out a coin, deftly flicking it to Randall. "Why don't you take these young ladies to get a soda, young man. As much as I would love to go with you, this work just won't wait."

He tipped his hat to all three and continued down the sidewalk.

"Unreal," Nadia said. "I just met the president."

"He isn't president yet," Randall said. "Look at this, it's a Liberty Head." He turned the coin in his hands, studying the front and the back. "You heard the man," he said. "Let's get a soda. Follow me."

He crossed the street and walked to a bus stop. When a bus came, he entered through the back doors, slipping in as passengers left. The girls followed and got on behind him.

"Just get ready to jump off," he told them.

They rode the bus two blocks before the driver took any notice of them. Randall saw the driver's scowl in the rear-view mirror. At the next stop the doors opened and he hopped out, pulling June by the sleeve. Nadia was a step behind.

"Come on," he said, walking quickly away. It wasn't long before he spotted what he was looking for. The Walgreen's sign acted as a magnet for him. A smaller sign hung below, lit in neon: Fountain Lunch. He pushed open the door and entered. He walked past racks of tobacco and cigarettes, glass counters displaying perfumes, and tables with stacks of soaps. Handbags hung on a rack. Magazines stood in a corner. In the back corner he saw the counter he was looking for. A bar jutted out from the wall with almost a dozen stools mounted in front of it. A black man in a white jacket and white hat was drying glasses at the far end. Randall sat down and put the coin on the counter. June and Nadia sat to each side.

"*Now for a real treat!*" he said. He picked up menu cards and handed one to each girl. "*You heard the man,*" he said. "*Time to enjoy a soda. Choose something from the fountain.*"

Nadia read the menu: "*Sodas mixed to perfection with ice cream and topped with whipped cream.*" Randall waved to the man behind the counter with his menu. The man put down his dish towel and walked over to the three.

"*What can I get you fine young people?*" he asked.

"*Three sodas, please,*" said Randall. "*I'd like the chocolate marshmallow. How about you June?*"

"*I have no idea,*" she said.

"*And June will have the crushed cherry,*" he said. "*That's appropriate.*"

"*And what would the young lady like?*" the server asked, looking at Nadia.

"*What would you recommend?*" she asked.

"*My favorite is the butterscotch nut, if you like butterscotch. But who doesn't like butterscotch?*" he added with a smile.

"*That sounds fine,*" Nadia said. "*Butterscotch nut, thank you.*"

"*My pleasure,*" he said. "*I'll be right back.*"

Nadia watched as he went to the fountain and picked up a tall tapered glass. He pumped in some chocolate, went to the soda jerk and poured in the carbonated water, he gave it a little stir, and finished it with a stream of milk. He added a scoop of ice cream and sprinkled it with small marshmallows. He placed it front of Randall. "*I'll be right back with your drinks, ladies,*" he said before returning to the fountain.

Randall took a sip from the straw sticking out of his drink. "*This is too much,*" he said.

"*What is your problem?*" Nadia asked. "*You act like this is some sort of game or something.*"

"Hey," Randall said. "Nothing of the sort. I'm just enjoying the moment. Look at this! This is absolutely delicious. Want a taste?"

"What the fuck is your problem?" Nadia asked.

"Easy Nadia, not so loud. Listen. She wanted us to be here. She wanted us to see the stadium, to bump into Wallace." He took a long sip from his straw.

The man behind the counter brought June her soda, then Nadia's. "I hope you enjoy," he said before returning to the end of the bar.

"She hasn't told us what our assignment is yet, but it has to involve all this. She said we were going to help elect a President, and I think we just met him. She'll tell us the details when it's time. Let's just enjoy this while we can. That's all I'm saying." Randall took a long sip of his drink.

"She messes with us big time and you want to have an ice cream soda? What the fuck is she doing, Randall?" Nadia whispered.

"She'll tell us soon, I'm sure of it," Randall said. "She doesn't do anything by accident. She wanted us to see the stadium. She wanted us to meet the President. She no doubt knew he would be walking right where he was and when he was. She didn't leave me money like she usually does, you know. Maybe she even knew he would give us this," he said.

"Wallace isn't President yet, you heard him," Nadia said.

"Maybe that's part of it then." Randall fingered the coin. "Amazing what this can buy here," he said.

"Quit playing with the coin, Randall. What do think she wants us to do?" Nadia asked.

"I don't know yet. But don't worry, she'll tell us. In the meantime, let's just relax and take advantage of where we are."

June stared at the tall glass in front of her, bubbles rising through flavored water, ice cream melting on the surface. She pushed it away and stood up. "Fuck you, Randall," she said, walking away without looking back.

"*She has a point, you know,*" *Nadia said, looking at the abandoned drink. She stood and walked to the man behind the corner.* "*Thank you very much,*" *she said.*

"*My pleasure,*" *he answered.* "*You have yourself a real nice day.*"

Nadia smiled at him, turned and walked out of the shop, leaving Randall sitting at the counter to finish his soda.

*N*adia left the store and walked towards the city. She paused in front of the stadium, watching workmen putting up banners and replacing awnings. A crowd gathered around the entrance. Some people carried stacks of placards and boxes. Others gawked at the building, the wide eyed and open-mouthed look of the tourist. Even they were well dressed. A group of black women emerged from the stadium and Nadia crossed the street. She followed as they made their way down Madison, walking just behind. Those at the rear of the group smiled at her, but nothing more. Their excited chatter floated back to her.

After a few blocks Nadia turned down a side street and continued to walk. Before long trees lined the street. A waist high fence surrounded a large area of green. Nadia walked through a gate and over cut grass. A wide path wound its way past shrubbery and she followed it. Trees planted along the path provided shade. Along the path benches were placed at intervals.

Nadia sat at one. A couple strolled past, holding hands and intent on each other. Nadia closed her eyes and listened to nearby birds. Doves cooed. Pigeon wings swished through the air, moving ungainly bodies from tree to tree. A blackbird called from a branch. She relaxed, her mind quieting. She began to drift into the silence, but intuitively opened *her eyes. It was too quiet. The birds were silent. A Southside instinct kicked in. She wasn't alone.*

Without moving her head, Nadia scanned the area in front of her. She looked at nearby trees and through bushes. Finally turning her head, she saw him. A man in a grey tweed suit was standing down the path, looking her way. When their eyes met, he began to walk towards her. As he neared, he indicated the bench.

"May I?" he asked.

Nadia said nothing. She quickly scanned the area. Path into more cover, short fence to the rear, open grass to the left. Her black leather shoes were not ideal for running, and probably prone to slip. The fence was jumpable, but the damned dress might get hung up.

"You're OK," he said. "I just want to talk." He took off his felt hat to reveal badly cut short hair.

"What are you, some kind of S-O?" Nadia asked.

"I don't know what that means," he said.

"Security Officer. Cop. Police."

"No, I'm not a policeman. But I do want to ask you about somebody," he said.

Nadia kept an eye on the man beside her while choosing the best escape route with her peripheral vision.

"I'm looking for somebody, that's all. Someone who doesn't belong here," he said. He could see Nadia tense.

"Not like that," he said. "I see three young people leave a building on West Madison. Sometimes you leave together, at other times you leave in pairs. The person I'm looking for never comes outside. Who is it? Who is inside that building?"

"What's she to you?" Nadia asked.

"Who is 'she'?" he replied.

Nadia looked away, at the nearby street, wishing it were closer.

"It's OK," he said. "Like I told you, I only want to talk. You don't have to do that tough girl act."

"If you're not a cop, why are you asking so many questions?"

"That's a long story, for another time," he said. "The young man among you, is he attached to her in some way? He seems different from you and the other girl. More experienced."

"You were outside the cafe! Why are you following us?" Nadia asked.

"I told you, I'm looking for her, not you. I think she wants you to do something that might get you into trouble. Maybe do something that shouldn't happen. I can see from your reaction that you know what I'm talking about. Anything you can tell me that can help, that's all I want. I'm worried about her ... intentions. I don't think she means well," he s aid.

Nadia began to inch away. He stood slowly and raised his hands, one open, the other still holding his hat. He stepped back from the bench and away from the girl. He took another step backward.

"Think about it," he said. "I'll talk to you later. And be careful. Believe it or not, not everybody is out to get you." He put his hat on, gave a weak smile, turned and walked away.

When he was out of sight, Nadia quickly left the park. She followed street after street, changing direction and looking over her shoulder often, until she found a better place to close her eyes and try to wake up.

21

"Good morning, my heroes," Miss Beil said.

"Good morning, Cassy," Randall answered.

Miss Beil glanced at June and Nadia. "Good morning, Cassey," they both said.

"Very good. Before we start, we have some unpleasant business to take care of," Miss Beil said, looking at Nadia. "It seems that one of you has been talking to somebody they shouldn't be talking to. I didn't think I had to tell you that when you leave this room you do not talk to strangers. The world is full of strangers, dangerous strangers who might want to interfere." Miss Beil stood up from her desk and walked towards the three with her ruler in hand. Each student stared down at their desks as she walked among them.

"After today you will each know who you need to speak with, and what you will need to do. There was a swish as the wooden ruler cut through the air, followed by a loud slap as it connected with skin.

June let out a loud cry and clutched her face. She cried out again but quickly stifled any more noise. Randall and Nadia could only hear her breathing heavily, sniffling and moving in her seat. Nadia peeked out of the corner of her eyes, surprised it wasn't she that received the blow. Miss Beil stood above June. She reached down and stroked the girl's hair gently.

"June will pull herself together while we get started. Such a pretty thing. She cares so much about her face." Miss Beil looked down at the girl. "And June, you will be needing that pretty face of yours quite soon, so please take good care of it. Use your sleeve to wipe away that snot, dear. And stay away from strangers."

Miss Beil walked to the blackboard at the front of the room where she drew a tree consisting of naked branches reaching out from a thick trunk. She started talking without turning around.

"Each and every world is like a branch. They grow out of the trunk, the essence of everything. You notice, here, how the branch splits and another begins to grow out of it, going in its own direction?" She circled a fork in a branch she had just drawn. "Have you ever wondered why a branch might just … branch out wherever it does? No? I don't imagine you ever have. What is probably the most important question is not why it might branch off, but how. They both go together, actually. Why and how, how and why."

She turned around and looked at the three sitting and watching her. "Eyes to the front please," she said before turning back to the board.

"Look at the circle again. It is the point where it is all possible. Some of these points can lead to a large new growth. Others might struggle, whither, and even die. Yes, I like this analogy. You can simply look at any tree and see exactly what I am talking about. But what I want to draw your attention to is the circle. It is the point of possibility. These points are possibilities. They are opportunities," Miss Beil set down her chalk, dusted her hands, and sat down at her desk.

"You are here, Randall, June, and Nadia, to take advantage of an opportunity. You are here to ensure that a branch is able to grow. As this branch grows strong, I grow strong. It is the branch you wake up on. Oh," she said smiling, "another little picture! Three little birds perched on their branch. You are here because if that branch does not grow …

well. Let me just say, it would not be good. We must nurture it. We must protect it. We must ensure that it sprouts at just the right place."

"I am sure those two don't have a clue what might be going on outside, but Nadia, what do you think?" Miss Beil asked.

"A party convention?"

"Good girl. Flags and buntings, crowds of out of towners. And you met a gentleman outside, I believe? What did you think of that tall man you met in front of the stadium, Nadia?"

"He seemed nice," Nadia said.

"Don't be flippant, Nadia. Answer the question."

Nadia bit her lip and looked at her desk, "I think he was a good President. That he tried," she said. "He had the people in mind, not just rich folks like all the rest. Yeah, I think that he was a good man."

"Yes, I agree. He certainly was that. But you look pensive, Nadia," Miss Beil said. "What is it? Tell the class."

Nadia looked at June and Randall. "Well," she said, "he isn't President yet. You heard him outside. When I called him that he laughed. He said, 'not yet'. This is the convention."

Miss Beil clapped her hands slowly. "Very well done, Nadia. Your civics teacher must be so proud of you. What do you remember about the conference? Anybody? Nadia?"

"I'm sorry, I don't remember much. We didn't spend too long on it. It was the last of its kind. Parties chose their candidates differently afterwards."

"OK. True. Anybody else?"

"There was a fire," Randall said.

"Yes, Randall, there was a fire," Miss Beil smiled at him, "there was indeed."

Miss Beil walked towards her three students and moved a desk directly in front of them. She squeezed into it and faced them.

"*Now, my little birds, my heroes, we come to your assignments. Each of you will have very important work to do in the coming days. Very important work. There are many who don't want you to succeed. Your work will not be easy, but I know you are ready for it.*"

She looked at each in turn, unsmiling, boring into their eyes with a cold gaze. "I will speak to you each in turn, giving special instructions as to what is required. I will start with Nadia, our bright member with special skills. Randall, be a star and take June somewhere nice."

Miss Beil frowned at Randall, "treat her special and be a gentleman. You are with a lady now. A beautiful young woman. She is a rose among thorns when she is in our company. If I hear you have acted otherwise, I will not be happy."

Randall nodded. He and June got up and went to the door.

"And, my little birds," Miss Beil said. "Don't talk to strangers."

N adia watched June and Randall leave. The door closed with a click as it locked. She turned to see Miss Beil smiling at her.

"You are a clever girl. Have you figured out why you are here yet?" she asked. "No, I can see you haven't. Show me your arm."

Nadia hesitated, glanced at her arm, and slowly lifted it towards Miss Beil.

Miss Beil laughed. "Relax dear. I just want you to notice the color. There are certain places a person like you can't go. There are places a person like you shouldn't go. The country club. The better neighborhoods. The front of the bus. But for our purposes, that skin of yours will prove very useful—who you'll meet, why you'll blend right in. You'll be among your own."

The muscles in Nadia's jaw clenched as she stared at Miss Beil, who still wore a smile. Miss Beil walked to her desk, opened the drawer, and took out a jar. She placed it on the desktop. Watching Nadia tense, she pushed the jar to the side.

"I'm sure that won't be necessary," she said.

"I'm sorry, Miss Beil," Nadia said.

"Please, Nadia," Miss Beil said. "Call me Cassy." Miss Beil picked up her chair and carried it to Nadia. She placed it in front of her and sat down.

"As I said, you're a smart girl and you know what I'm talking about. Go on, dear."

"The Black Caucus," Nadia said.

"Exactly. Congressman Dawson will be there. William Levi Dawson, himself. Your daddy, no doubt, had a picture of him, alongside his pictures of Frederick Douglas and Marcus Garvey. But they were all confiscated, weren't they?" Miss Beil asked.

Nadia remained silent, studying the woman in front of her. White skin, light freckles on her cheeks, blond hair, chest rising and falling as she breathed, moist lips painted red. Nadia's vision began to blur and Miss Beil began to move and change, turn into something fiercer, larger, even more menacing. Nadia blinked and her vision cleared. Miss Beil sat in front of her in her white dress and continued to speak.

"For Dawson to save the day he will need help. That help will be you. That wonderful moment when Dawson interrupts the proceedings and nominates Wallace for Vice President—oh, goosebumps, see?" she held her arm out. Nadia saw smooth skin. Miss Beil rose and went back to her desk, reached into the drawer and withdrew a knife. She brought it back to Nadia and set it on the desktop in front of her.

"This is how you will protect him," she said. "Call it security. Any obstacle in his way, you will clear it. You probably won't even have to use it, just wave it in a demented manner, or slash away, ruin a suit or two. That should be enough. If it isn't, you just have to do more. You'll do what you have to, because you will not shirk what you are here to do. Dawson will make it to the podium at the right time, and your daddy will have his hero. What an exciting role you will play!"

Miss Beil pushed her chair back to stand. She put her hands on her hips.

"Your skin isn't your only asset, Nadia," she said. "You have skills I am interested in. Very useful skills. I watched during your first visit to

class. It is why you are a member of our class. Why you will always be a member of class. The things we can achieve!"

Miss Beil picked up the knife, "you will practice now. Put your hands on your desk."

Nadia looked up at the woman holding the knife. "Do it," Miss Beil said. "Put your finger through the desk. Go on. We haven't time to waste."

Nadia looked at her finger and slowly pressed it down. It began to disappear into the desktop until it was buried up to the second knuckle. Miss Beil bent over and saw the tip of Nadia's finger protruding from the underside. She stood and clapped her hands.

"Wonderful, Nadia, Wonderful. Keep going!"

Nadia let her finger sink in up to the top, then slowly withdrew it. She repeated the exercise.

Miss Beil clapped again, "now your hand. Do your hand!"

Nadia laid her hand flat on the surface and gently pressed. It sunk into the wood until all that was showing was the stump of her wrist. She looked at Miss Beil who nodded encouragement. Nadia pressed harder and her arm slipped through the wood up to the elbow. She slowly pulled it out and examined her hand.

"Do you know how you can do that?" Miss Beil asked.

"This is a dream," Nadia said.

"But you know it is real, you can feel it," Miss Beil replied. "Do the wall," she commanded.

Nadia rose and walked to the nearest wall. She placed her hand on it, looked at Miss Beil, and gently pushed. Her hand gradually disappeared into the plaster. She pulled it out and looked at it, placed it back on the wall and watched it disappear. Miss Beil clapped her hands.

"Good girl! Good Girl! Now, walk through the wall!"

"I can't," Nadia said.

"You don't know what you can't do yet. Walk through the wall, Nadia. Now!"

Miss Beil's excitement sent a shiver down Nadia's spine. She pressed her body against it. Her nose flattened against the cold plaster. She pressed harder. Her nose hurt. She stood flat against the surface. Finally, she stepped back. She studied the wall and looked at Miss Beil's expectant face. Nadia smiled. She turned around and faced away from the wall. Taking a step back she slowly entered the barrier. She took another small step, felt the air around her liquify. She closed her eyes and continued back. She thought of Jell-O, how she would squeeze it in her hands when she was younger. Only her whole body was squeezing the Jell-O.

When Nadia opened her eyes, she saw the outside of the building. She quickly turned around and saw cars pass on the street in front of her. To the right the sidewalk was empty. To the left, a man was walking away. Nadia saw the door to the classroom. She tried the handle. It was locked. She knocked. A grinning Miss Beil opened the door and let her in.

"Wonderful!" she said. She walked to the center of the room and looked down. "Do the floor now," she said. "Do the floor!"

Nadia walked reluctantly towards her. She stood looking at her foot. She lifted her toes and set them back down. She pursed her lips, concentrating. A minute passed in silence.

"I can't," she said.

Miss Beil looked disappointed, but only briefly. She smiled again, "now I am excited. I so look forward to the work we will be doing. We are destined to have such a wonderful future together."

"But first things first, Nadia. There's work to be done."

June smelled flowers. The odor of freshly cut grass filled the air. The sun warmed her skin, and a light breeze caressed her face. She sat with her eyes closed, holding the moment just a little bit longer. She leaned back, reached blindly to the side and grasped an arm rest. She breathed deeply several times and opened her eyes.

A small flower bed lay in front of the park bench. Red, yellow, and pink zinnias mingled in colorful concert. Purple iris stood above them. Chrysanthemum, Dahlias, Daisies. June liked flowers. A large rhododendron bush lined the path, its purple petals carpeting the walk. A nearby pond attracted ducks who lazily paddled in the green water. Mature trees formed a canopy to provide cool shade on such a humid summer day.

June stood and looked at the park. She lifted a hand and examined her fingers, wrist, arm. She twirled and admired her dress, light green cotton reaching just past her knees, decorated with white flower patterns. A slim green belt showed a shapely waist and let the garment hang loosely on her hips. The neckline hung just low enough to reveal the smooth white skin of her chest, discreetly inviting the eye. She felt pretty.

June took a long look at the small park before leaving, a small green square surrounded by terraced houses. At the corner she caught a passing bus and made the short trip into the city.

***

"You're going to go on a little trip, June," Miss Beil said. "To a pleasant enough city. It's a bit provincial for my taste, but you won't be going to sight see. There's a man you need to meet. There's always a man. You'll do your special magic, little vixen that you are, and you'll make this man not only do anything you ask, but want to do anything you say. Men are so weak that way, so easy to manipulate."

Miss Beil walked around her desk and leaned against the one nearest to June.

"Listen closely, June," Miss Beil continued. "Don't just sit there looking gloomily at your hands. This is a man who is very important and who can cause a great deal of damage. You need to make sure that he doesn't have the opportunity. You will make sure that he doesn't, because it is very important to you. You know what will happen if you fail."

Miss Beil reached a hand towards June's face. June flinched and shut her eyes as the older woman stroked her cheek with the back of her fingers. Miss Beil talked as she paced in front of the desks.

"Mr. Robert Hannegan is an important man in the party. He has maneuvered himself to be the Party Chairman and will have a crucial role to play in the coming convention. All the party bosses have been busy plotting and scheming to get their man nominated. Everybody knows how sick the old man in the White House is," Miss Beil stuck her hand out and shook it. "Every time he hands something to anybody his hands tremble. Ask him for a drink if you want a little giggle. It's just a matter of time before he slips his mortal coil, and then the next in line assumes the throne. The vice president.

"This is a nasty little affair that's been going on for months so I'll just summarize for you. Democracy here is run by machines. In Missouri—yes, June, it is pronounced 'misery', even by those unfortunate enough to call it home—in Misery the machine is run by a fat, greedy old man named Pendergast. A short time ago, Pendergast put a nondescript little man named Truman into the Senate. And this Truman found his own rising star to mentor, Mr. Robert E. Hannegan. Isaac begat Eliphaz begat Zephon, ad nauseum. Stroking the ego or clutching onto coattails, whatever. The elder always has to have an apprentice. These types always reproduce like the insects they are.

"In his youth your Mr. Hannegan was an athlete. Professional football, professional baseball, there was nothing he couldn't do. Husky, strapping beast of a man—in his youth. Age has the tendency to settle around the waist and spill over the belt, to soften that strong jaw and add another neck. You get the picture, June, don't you?"

"Yes, Cassy," June said. Her eyes had returned to the desktop below her. A teardrop made a small wet mark on its surface.

"Now June, you just wipe those eyes. Mr. Robert Hannegan would have nothing to do with a silly little girl like you. He's much more into power than moist warm flesh," Miss Beil shook her head in sympathy. "His poor neglected Irma. His ticker isn't in the best of shape either—you'd probably kill him, and that just won't do.

"No, June, just like everybody else, Robert Hannegan has his own protege, a beautiful young man fresh out of law school, with that rare combination of ambition and smarts. He is who I want you to meet, dear. Old Bob really likes your young man. Maybe it's a father-son sort of thing, or he just knows that heart of his is going to pop and he wants a legacy. The human ego is so distasteful. I feel soiled speaking of it.

"What you are going to do is meet this young beau, court him, tease him, and then snare him. He needs to be tied around your little finger,

and you know what kind of knot is needed. At the convention he'll do whatever you ask," Miss Beil fluttered her eyelashes and laughed at June.

"I am so excited for you," she said. "This is what you're good at, June. It will be so fulfilling for you!"

24

The side doors opened and June stepped off the bus. The sidewalk filled with the lunch time rush. June entered on of the many shops surrounding the square. Shelves full of knick-knacks made the cramped space feel even more crowded. She smiled at the clerk and browsed for a few minutes. She picked up an ash tray with an image of a red bird catching a baseball. She felt the weight, rapped her knuckles against the bottom of the solid piece of glass. She set it back on the shelf and continued to browse.

Finally, she picked up a dinner sized plate. Holding it in both hands she lifted and examined its profile. She held it flat and tested its weight. It was made of porcelain, never intended for any real use. Its border was decorated with gold trim. A picture of a paddle steamer making its way down the river that flowed the length of the plate. An airplane rested in one corner, with Spirit of St. Louis proudly written below it. A red cardinal decorated another corner. A red, white, and blue flag waved along the bottom, with the Missouri state seal emblazoned in the center. The largest letters on the plate announced, 'St. Louis.'

June took the plate to the counter and paid the clerk for her souvenir. He wrapped it in delicate paper and she walked back onto the street. She headed straight for the courthouse, pausing briefly at the bottom of the steps. She opened her handbag and removed lipstick. She saw the young man hurrying down the stairs. She walked towards him, lifted her lipstick to her lips. He noticed the young woman too late and ran into her. The lipstick flew from her hand. The plate flew from the other. It hit the pavement and broke into over a dozen pieces. June stumbled and nearly fell, but he caught her just in time.

"Are you alright? I am so sorry," he said.

June caught her breath. "Yes, I think so," she said.

He held onto her arm and she leaned into him, knees weak. "Here, let me sit you down," he said. He guided her to a nearby bench and sat next to her, "are you sure you're OK? That was quite a fright."

"Yes," she said. "I just need to catch my breath."

"I think I broke something," he said. "Just wait here a moment." He quickly returned to the scene of the disaster and picked up pieces of the plate, returning with them wrapped in the torn paper.

"I don't think this will work anymore," he said.

"It was just a silly souvenir," June said.

"Still, I want to replace it. My name is Johnnie. Johnnie Vaughn," he gave her his hand. She took it and held it.

"I'm June. June Clavern."

"What a beautiful name. June. Pleased to meet you," Johnnie said. "I wish it could have been under better circumstances. How are you feeling?"

"I'm OK," she said, letting go of his hand.

"You have some ..." he gestured at her face. June took a small mirror out of her pocket and gasped. She licked a finger and wiped at the streak of red lipstick on her cheek.

"Here, let me," he said. He took a clean handkerchief out of his pocket and held it to her mouth. She moistened it and he gently wiped away the mark. She checked it with her mirror and smiled at him.

"Very nice," he said. June blushed. "I'm sorry," he said. "How about we start again without bumps and breaks? I was just going to celebrate with a drink. Come with me. It's the least I could do. Then we can replace this plate."

June studied his eyes, light blue and honest. "I'd like that," she said.

He stood up and offered his hand, which she gladly took. He frowned at the broken glass plate held in the other and put it in a nearby garbage can. Letting go of her hand he offered his elbow. "I know a really nice place just across the square. My lady?" he asked.

She put her arm through his. "Lead the way," she said.

He opened the door and June entered the first bar she had ever been in. Johnnie guided her to a small table and pulled the chair out for her. He waved to a waitress who quickly came to the table. He winked at June and said to the waitress, "two gimlets, please." Turning back to June he said, "let's have some fun. The drink matches your dress, which is lovely, by the way. Your dress, that is."

"Thank you," June said. She had heard creepy comments often before, but Johnnie's compliments seemed genuine.

When the drinks arrived, June looked at hers. "Gin, a spot of lime, with soda. I think you'll like it. Here, a toast," he raised his glass with June. "To Chicago," he said, "and the beautiful month of June."

June sipped her drink and nodded her approval. "Why Chicago, and this is July."

"Chicago," Johnnie said, "because that is where I will soon be. The case I was assigned to assist was just dismissed and I can accompany my boss to the party convention. And the month of June just because of its beautiful name."

"You're a lawyer?" June asked.

"Only just. I work for Rob Hannegan, an assistant of sorts, which means filing a lot of papers. As party chairman all his 'i's need dotting and 't's crossing."

"That sounds very important."

"Not as important as what our boys are doing in France right now," he said, looking into his drink.

June hesitated, but then placed her hand over his. "The country has to keep running here, too," she said before removing her hand.

"Tell me, what do you do in St. Louis, besides carry plates?"

"I'm just visiting my aunt," she said. "And the plate was a gift for my grandmother. She has never travelled very much."

"So where is home?" he asked.

"Chicago," she said.

"You live in Chicago? Well, that makes our little accident absolutely serendipitous," he smiled at June. "A happy accident. How long are you in town?"

"Just two more days," June said.

"Which is close to the time I'll be going there too. See, serendipity," he stared into her green eyes and noticed that she didn't look away. "Look, I don't mean to be forward, and I know we have just met, but I don't want to just buy you a plate and not see you again. Can I also buy you dinner tonight? I know a restaurant I think you'll really like and—"

"That would be very nice," June said.

"Swell," he said. "Let's get that plate and then I'll finish my day at the office, watching the arms of the clock slowly making their way to when I can see more of you."

He stood and offered June his arm again. They returned to the cramped shop and bought a second plate, agreed on a time to meet, and parted with a squeeze of the hand. June watched the young man walk away, not turning away until he was out of sight. She dumped the plate in the first garbage can she passed. She used more of the money Miss Beil gave her to find a nearby hotel and get ready for her date.

25

Johnnie met June with a modest bouquet of flowers. She held them close to her breast as he escorted her into the restaurant. A table was waiting for them. As soon as they sat a waiter brought over a bottle of wine. He poured a small portion in a glass which Johnnie swirled before tasting. He nodded and the waiter poured out two glasses. They both took a drink.

"How is the wine?" he asked after the waiter left.

"It's good," she said. "I don't usually drink wine."

"If you'd like something else—"

"No, this is nice. I like it," she said.

The waiter returned with menus but Johnnie stopped him. "If you don't mind?" he asked June. June smiled at him so he spoke to the waiter who nodded and left.

"You speak French?" June asked.

"Just enough to order a nice meal," he answered. "Tell me, how was your afternoon? No more accidents or broken plates?"

"None at all," June said. "I just took in some sights and bought a few more presents. How was your day?"

"Oh, dotting and crossing. There are a lot of last-minute details to deal with before the convention starts."

"It all sounds so important," June said.

He took a sip of his wine. "Let's not talk about work. Here we are, two people in a nice French restaurant, enjoying good wine and each other's company. Tell me about yourself, June. What are your dreams?"

Johnnie set his glass down and put his hand over June's. "I'm sorry," he said. "You look shocked. I don't mean to pry. I was only wondering what you want out of life."

"It's OK," she said. "Really, it is. Nobody has asked me that before."

"Skipping the small talk and getting right to the heart of it," he said. "That's probably moving too fast, I'm sorry."

"No, really, it's OK," June said. She turned her hand over and held Johnnie's. "I guess, if I was honest ..."

"Please do, always," he said.

"I want to be free," she said. "I mean, I want to be free to love and be loved, have a husband, and children ... what every woman wants, I guess. To be looked after and protected. To feel safe— "

The waiter came with their meal and they both took advantage of the interruption to look away.

"And you," June asked. "What are your dreams, Johnnie?"

"Well," he tried. "That is hard to follow. I mean, of course, I would like the same, to have that person waiting at home. But maybe not here. Have you ever been to DC? It's a wonderful city, there's so much history, and so much action. I would like to be in the thick of it. I think Bob is going to go far, and he can open a lot of doors. Sometimes I even think about public office .... You're laughing at me!"

"I'm not laughing. I'm smiling. It all sounds so wonderful," June said.

"It can be," he said. "But I can imagine that doing it alone would make it all empty. I see that from time to time, guys whose whole life is their work. If there is nobody to share your life with, what's the point?"

June felt a fluttering in her stomach, butterflies, nerves, whatever they might be called. And she enjoyed the feeling. She enjoyed sitting across from this young man with piercing yet gentle blue eyes, thick dark hair, and strong shoulders. She wasn't surprised when, after the plates were cleared, he told her he didn't want the evening to end.

"Me neither," she said. Almost too easy, Miss Beil would say.

They walked in the warm summer evening. Their hands brushed each other and he took hers in

his.

"My, that was brave," she said.

"Bravest thing I ever did," he told her. They walked closer until she was nuzzling into him and his arm went around her bare shoulders. Soon they were in front of his downtown apartment. He turned her towards him and kissed her.

"I'm sorry," he said, pulling slightly back. "I'd say that war makes everything move faster, but that just sounds like a ploy."

"Don't be sorry," she said. "I am exactly where I want to be."

He led her upstairs and into his small studio. It was clean and orderly. He guided her to the small settee. She stood as he approached her and they kissed again, deeper and longer. He pulled her close. His hand found the zipper at the back of her dress and he slowly moved it down. June wriggled her shoulders free and the dress fell to her feet. He picked her up and carried her to the small bed.

Afterwards, June held him, spent, in her arms. She made excuses about getting back to her aunt's. He coaxed her into enjoying more time together, moments that June didn't want to end. He walked her downstairs and hailed a cab. She turned in the back seat as the cab drove her away, watching him recede. He gazed back until the cab was out of sight. They would make plans about meeting up in Chicago when they saw each other the next day.

"Like a fiddle, my dear, you'll play him like a fiddle," Miss Beil had told her. Only June wasn't playing.

26

Nadia's mother stood in the bedroom doorway watching her daughter sleep. Weeks had passed since Nadia's arrest, weeks of what the state deemed 'therapy', weeks of medication for a condition she knew her daughter didn't have. Weeks of watching her daughter struggle through each night, afraid to sleep, tormented in her dreams when she did.

When presented with the choice of believing a court appointed therapist or her own daughter, she never wavered. If Nadia said her dreams were real, then they were real. Her mother grew up with her nan's stories. Ruby would gather her grandchildren at her feet and tell them about other times and faraway places. Pictures painted in her grandchildren's imaginations, of African kingdoms, proud warriors, a land of gold, great cities. Nadia's mother smiled, remembering one name: Timbuktu. She frightened them with harrowing memories of horrific, cramped ships full of dying people, slave markets, beatings. She told them about distant families, who lost their names and their freedom on those ships.

Ruby told them to use their dreams. To learn about their people. But although she loved hearing her nan's stories, Nadia's mother was too frightened. She touched another world once, at least she thought she did. A dream where she was aware that she was dreaming, in a world that felt very real. A tree, an invitation. But her fear got the better of her and she retreated back into the safety of forgetfulness. And she had life's demands—a baby to raise, a husband to mourn, a cause to fight. She tried to protect her daughter, as much as she could. Teach her how to be a negro child in this white, patriarchal, and evangelical America. How to stay alive. To always be on her guard. When stopped by the S-O to stay calm, don't fight back, don't talk back, don't make eye contact, do what they say. Your life is what's important, don't let them take that too. She could see her husband in Nadia's face, especially her mouth. That smile that was part smirk. The quick rebut. She wanted to make sure it didn't get her daughter killed, like it did her husband.

But now Nadia was being tormented by something else, something she couldn't understand. She was tired of watching, helpless. If she couldn't protect her daughter while she slept, she could use her waking hours. She walked to Nadia's bed, reached down and gently shook her shoulder.

"Wake up, Nadia," she said.

Nadia opened her eyes and sighed.

"Come on, girl, get yourself up and ready," her mother said. "We're going out."

"What's the matter?" Nadia asked.

"We've got some work to do. I'll give you a few minutes to get ready," she said. "I've got a few calls to make. We'll grab a bite on the street."

Nadia stretched slowly and watched her mother leave the room. She climbed out of bed, put on some clothes, and went into the bathroom.

When she came out, she saw her mother take several phones out of her purse. She selected one and dialed a number. When it was answered she spoke briefly.

"Hey Drew, there's some things we gotta know. See you shortly."

She hung up, and dialed again. "Dion, my man. Yeah, I know. Got my kitten in tow on a research trip, cool? Great." She hung up and dialed once more.

"Jam. Might stop by, OK? Cool."

She took the sim card out of the phone and bent it until it broke. She put the remaining phones back in her bag and noticed Nadia staring. Reaching in she took a phone out and tossed it to her daughter. "Keep that in your pocket, OK? It's not a good look to get stopped with a bag full of burners."

"What's up?" Nadia asked.

"I'm tired of being helpless," her mother said. "It's time we did a little research into this Miss Beil. Maybe we'll find something that will help. I've got some friends at cyber cafés we can use."

"Can't we just use your computer?" Nadia asked.

"You know better than that, Nadia," her mother said. "Every search is monitored. I don't want to attract any more attention to this place."

Before Nadia could reply her mother opened the door of the house. Nadia quickly slipped on her shoes and followed her into the street. Her mother threw the phone she had used into the first garbage can they passed. They walked for several blocks as Nadia spoke about her dream, of putting her hand in the desk and walking through a wall.

Finally, her mother stopped at a cyber cafe. Posters and flyers pasted to the front windows made it hard to see in and added gloom to the interior. Nadia's mother nodded to the young man behind a counter near the entrance. He smiled at her and handed her two small slips of paper. She gave one to her daughter. A log in name and password. Nadia followed her mother as she headed towards two computers near the back of the shop and sat in front of one. Nadia sat next to her.

"We'll only have about 20 minutes once a keyword triggers an alarm. So search quickly. I'll start with some history. Why don't you start with the bitch?"

Nadia stared at her mother, who was already typing. Nadia logged on and tried a search. Cassy Beil. Images of women appeared, none looking like Miss Beil. She tried variations of the name: Cassandra, Kassy, Cassi, Cassie. There were people who had the name, but none was the person she wanted. Nadia tried removing letters and spaces: CassyBeil, , KassyBeil. "Did you mean ..." She tried shortening the name: CasyBeil. She tried it with 'K'. She typed too fast and missed the ' y' and mixed some letters.

Nadia leaned closer to the screen. Kazbiel. A Norwegian band, playing something called 'Death Metal.' The web page was stamped with the typical warning on anything foreign and deemed subversive in the Land of the Free. Nadia didn't click on the link, which would trigger an alarm somewhere. Besides, she knew Miss Beil wasn't a band. She scrolled down and stopped. This time she opened the link. It was an approved site. A dictionary of angels.

Kasbiel: (Kaspiel—' sorcery'), referred to as "chief of the oath," whose original name was Biqa, meaning "good person." But Kasbiel fell, and after his fall he was renamed Kazbiel, meaning "he who lies to God."

"Anything?" her mother asked.

"I don't know," Nadia said. "Weird stuff. She's either a banned Scandinavian rock band or a fallen angel. I can almost believe the last one. But I had to spell her name all wrong to get anything."

Her mother pushed her chair back and stood. "Time to move, kid." She waved at the front counter and they walked to the back of the shop. Opening the door, they stepped into the alley behind it. They made their way to the next internet cafe. Inside were similar rows of computers. Dirty, worn carpet. Walls with fading paint. Just enough notices stuck on the windows to obscure the view. Customers sat with headphones and backs turned toward the door. Most were gaming. "That's another type of drug," her father had said. "It's easy to control a population that doesn't even go outside. Might as well be shooting heroin." A girl Nadia's age handed her mother two small slips of paper. Her mother continued past the counter towards the back of the shop. The girl smiled at Nadia as she followed her mother.

Nadia's mother didn't speak but started her search where she left off. Nadia looked at her keyboard. Jacob Iverson, she typed. It was a popular name, but no one matched the man with long blond hair she had recently met. She tried it with a 'k'. A university professor, a professional baseball player, hits in languages she couldn't read, but no matches. Maybe he was from a different reality. It was hardly possible not to show up somewhere on the web.

Nadia stared at her keyboard again and typed her father's name: Jayden Ifedi.

"Radical shot at checkpoint" she read. "Security officers shot and killed the negro radical Jayden Ifedi at a mobile checkpoint. Officers report Ifedi approached the checkpoint carrying concealed items believed to be weapons. After refusing repeated demands to cease his advance officers took defensive measures in self-defense. Ifedi, a dissident journalist and longtime suspected member of the Negro Liberation Movement ..."

Nadia scrolled down and found similar stories. She tried another search: writings by Jayden Ifedi. A white screen with red letters answered her. "You have requested a page that is no longer available," it read.

"Nadia, what are doing?" her mother whispered.

"I just wanted to see—"

"Fuck! Sorry, Hun. It's time we went. That was sure to attract attention." She frowned and shrugged to the girl behind the counter. Nadia followed her mother once again out a back door and into an alley. They moved quickly, emerging onto a side street and blending into the people on the sidewalk.

"Nadia, we can't waste keywords if we're going to make any sense of this."

"I know, I just wanted to see."

"You're not going to see anything useful there. Let's try one more place. No need to push our luck or endanger friends. Can you focus this time?"

"Yes," Nadia answered.

27

They entered another shop. A man with long dreadlocks greeted her mother with a hug and offered a hand to Nadia. No names were exchanged, only small slips of paper. She found herself in front of another old computer with a dirty keyboard. Nadia typed in 'William Levi Dawson'. Born in Albany, Georgia in 1886. Studied law at Northwestern before the first world war. Served as a lieutenant in the 366th Infantry, a segregated regiment. He returned to Chicago after the war, practicing law until entering politics. Elected to congress in 1943, he was the first negro to hold a Cabinet level position, serving in the short-lived administration of Henry Wallace. After Wallace left the White House, Dawson's political career came to an abrupt end. He returned to law, challenging segregationist policies until he died of pneumonia shortly before his 70th birthday. He was admired by some, but hated by many.

The convention was well covered. Roosevelt was still president, but he was unable to attend due to his health. Everybody at the convention, at least the power brokers, knew that in choosing who would run on the ticket as Vice President, they were really picking the next president. Wallace was the sitting VP, probably the second most popular politician in the country, but the party bosses didn't like him. They didn't approve of his support of labor, his ideas about capitalism, his talk about a '*Century of the Common Man*.' To the political machine he was seen as more of a threat than an asset. The clear plan was to use the convention to nominate a more pliable hack, like Truman from Missouri, or even a southern racist like Byrnes. After the first vote, which Wallace easily won, the party bosses tried to call the session to a close and plan for the following day. They would never forgive the 'upstart negro' who spoiled their plans. Dawson reached the podium in time to call a second vote and Wallace won the nomination. That night the stadium where the convention was held burned to the ground, and the convention was forced to conclude with Wallace on the ticket.

Nadia's mother patted her leg. They both rose and exited through the rear of the shop and into an alley. She walked silently beside her mother as they returned to the street. They turned and pretended to window shop as an S-O Humvee drove past. At a restaurant Nadia's mother went and selected a booth. She held up two fingers and the waitress brought mugs of coffee and menus before returning to the counter.

"I don't get it," her mother said. "You say she wants you to help Dawson. She wants Wallace to be president. But that's what happened."

"When I'm there it hasn't happened yet. She says we need to protect the present, that we have to help him, make sure—"

"And his presidency was a disaster. His own party stabbed him in the back and undermined his administration every chance they got ..."

Nadia knew the history; she *had* read the text. When the war could end by dropping the new atomic bomb Wallace hesitated. While he saw the value in using bombs to demonstrate US power, he didn't want to kill thousands. But the military did it anyway. Two cities were obliterated, hundreds of thousands died horribly, and the war ended.

Wallace's authority never recovered. The generals took credit for the victory. The party bosses made sure Byrnes was nominated in '48 and Wallace returned to his farm in Iowa. General Douglas MacArthur's landing in Inchon sent the North Koreans retreating, marching all the way to the northern border. When the communist Chinese crossed the Yalu River the atomic bomb dropped on Harbin sent them quickly back with their tails tucked firmly between their legs. MacArthur's triumph made him unstoppable at home as well, and a landslide in '52 put him in the White House. Two terms later his VP, Richard Milhouse Nixon, succeeded him and the '60s rolled on. Vietnam was reunited after what happened in Hanoi. Latin American revolutionaries learned what was acceptable in Washington's backyard, and the American homeland was made safe from any 'un-American activities', like labor rights or integrationist subversion. Reagan, the Bushes, and then the billionaires followed.

It was a proud American century, Christian, patriotic and loyal. One nation under God.

"I still don't get it, Nadia," her mother said. "Does any of this help?"

"I don't know," Nadia said. "No. Maybe. I—" Nadia wiped her eyes.

"You can't believe what you read about your dad online, Nadia. You know that." Her mother lowered her voice, "they just shot him. He was in the wrong place at the wrong time, all he was doing was trying to get home before curfew. What you read are lies. But I don't have to tell you that, do I?"

"No," Nadia said. "Mom, are you NLM?"

They both sat silently as the waitress set their food on the table.

"Let's give it a rest for a little while. Eat your burger before it gets cold. Then we'll do something fun. Sometimes it helps just to stop thinking. Then we'll figure something out. There has to be a solution."

28

"Nadia, all the dreams you have shared with me are in the past, about things that have already happened. I find that very interesting, don't you?" Foskett flicked through his notes, pretending to look for something. Nadia didn't answer right away.

"Interesting isn't the word I would use. No, I don't find it interesting."

"What I mean is that ... well, what you mention ... what you talk about are all people in books, or ..." He saw Nadia clench her fists, "please, let me explain. I'm not doubting you or dismissing what you are experiencing."

"You are doubting me," Nadia said.

"Please, Nadia, let me explain," Foskett rose from behind his desk and sat on a chair facing Nadia. "There's something I would like to try," he said. "I want you to dream about the future ..."

"How can I do that?" Nadia asked. "I dream what she wants me to dream, where and when she wants me to dream—"

"Cassy Beil," Foskett said.

"Yeah, Cassy Beil. I close my eyes and fall asleep and she is there. I can't get away from her. She has power—"

"Which is why I want to try something different. Let me explain, at least," Foskett said.

"Do I have a choice? She has power, you have power, my teachers have power, those S-O fuckers have power. Everybody but me has ..."

"You do have a choice, Nadia. If you don't want to do it, you won't have to do it," Nadia sat silently looking at Foskett.

He waited a few moments before continuing. "What I would like to try is to induce a dream state through hypnosis. It helps access the subconscious, that part of your mind we're not aware of, but that influences us more than we want to admit. It's where we bury all of our traumas and fears, all of our hurt. That's why going there can be so healing. All of the material in our subconscious is the fuel for our dreams."

"Just tell me what you want to do," Nadia said.

Foskett leaned forward. "I want to take you to that place of dreams, to use a hypnotherapy technique to guide you there. It is perfectly safe. You'll be able to wake or end the session whenever you want to. We agree on a safe word, whatever you choose, and when you say it, whatever you experience will end and you'll be back here."

"What do I have to do?" Nadia asked.

"Just relax, and I'll guide you. That's all you really need to do—relax and let go."

"OK."

"You can stay on the sofa if you want—"

"I said, OK. You can start. Just do it already," Nadia said. "It's gotta be better than all the talk-talk we usually do."

"Good. Just sit comfortably, lie down or lean back, take off your shoes if you want," Nadia undid her laces and removed her shoes. She reclined on the couch.

"Now, close your eyes and relax. Breathe deeply three or four times. As you exhale, let all your tension flow out through your feet."

Nadia opened her eyes and looked at Foskett. He smiled at her, "It's OK. This is how we start. Have you thought of a safe word?"

"No. Yes. 'Dad'. Let's just make it 'dad'," she said.

"Good. When you say dad, we'll end the session. Feel your dad's arms around you, holding you safely when you say the word. When we end the session, I'll count back from five and talk you right back here. OK?"

"OK," she answered.

"Now close your eyes, and breathe," Foskett instructed.

Nadia did as she was instructed. With each exhalation she felt her body relax and settle into the sofa.

"Draw your attention to the top of your head," Foskett said softly. "Relax your scalp muscles. With every exhale, feel all the tension leave your scalp. Now relax your forehead ... your cheeks ... your jaw. Let all tension leave your jaw. Feel your jaw muscles loosen, feel the softness there as any tension flows away, emptying your body of anxiety and blocks."

Foskett continued to guide Nadia through the parts of her body, down the back of her torso and legs, starting again with the front of her body, her neck, chest, abdomen, legs. He guided her down her spine, vertebrae by vertebrae. Finally, he guided her back to her eyes.

"When you are totally relaxed, Nadia, I am going to ask you to open your eyes," he said. "Try to open your eyes, Nadia."

Foskett noticed a very slight movement beneath Nadia's eyelids, but her eyes remained closed. "Now imagine a place in the future. Not too far in the future. Five years, or ten years. Picture the place, a place you know, a nearby place. Look at the building you are standing beside. Look down the street. Listen to any sound. Feel the air on your skin. Smell the street. Pay attention to the details around you. Now, Nadia, raise your hand and look at it."

29

Nadia looked at her hand. She followed the lines of her palm. She saw the back of her fingers. Nadia turned her hand over and studied her great nan's ring on her finger, a simple gold band with three small diamonds. She was wearing the same clothes she had worn to Foskett's office, a simple yet modest summer dress. The laces on her shoes were untied.

Nadia was on a street that she knew. She had walked down it many times. It was dirtier, but it was still the same street. A pile of garbage sat stinking on the opposite side. Uncollected black bags of refuse. Trash spilled from holes ripped by dogs or rats or some other hungry animal. The air reeked. Further down a burnt-out car still smoldered. Nadia heard an explosion in the distance and saw smoke rising over buildings in the distance. The growl of a Humvee made her instinctively step into the shadow of a doorway. The vehicle sped past, the S-O inside not noticing her through the tinted windows.

"That's Englewood burning," a voice at Nadia's feet said. Nadia pushed herself against the far wall, away from the voice.

"They'll just kill some more negros and go back to business."

"What are you talking about?" Nadia asked.

"The riots. Another 'race riot'. Or call it an insurrection, like the NLM prefer. Same thing. Another massacre," the voice was slurred, as if the speaker's tongue was having difficulty with the simplest movement. Nadia tried to make out a face in the shadow. A man readjusted a dirty blanket and tried to sit up straighter. He settled for slumping against the stair above him.

"Compton's been razed to the ground. They brought in jet fighters. Napalm or whatever it's called. Just a fuckin' massacre. Razing their own fucking cities. Pardon my French. South Philly .... South Philly, man. But they ain't gonna tell us shit. It's just all shit. They'll drop another bomb on Russia and then we're all fucked anyway, 'cause the Russians will fire back this time, and not just with one. That fucking Armageddon the Believers want so bad. Think the more shit they blow up their precious Christ will return. Dumb fucks," the man stopped speaking and stared at the garbage across the street.

He turned his attention back to his own doorway and peered at Nadia. He narrowed his eyes. "I know you," he said. "You ..."

Nadia leaned closer to get a better look. His eyes were bloodshot. His face was dirty and bloated and it had been days or even weeks since he had shaved. His long, matted hair was peppered with grey.

"Mr. Foskett?" she asked.

"Mr.," he laughed. "You're Nadia. Nadia. Nadia. Nadia. Leave Nadia alone, she said. Keep your distance, she said. Do not pry, I am not to be taken casually, she said. But she did it anyway. Every night, whatever I did. Whatever I—"

"What are you talking about? What's happened to you?"

Foskett laughed, "you happened to me!" He wiped his mouth with a dirty sleeve. "As soon as you came to my office. Every time I slept, she would be there. Do you know what she wanted? For me to leave you alone. Didn't want me asking, didn't want me listening. That's why we would just sit there, session after session, hour after hour, staring at the walls."

"I don't remember just sitting there," Nadia said.

"No, you were a regular little chatterbox until I made you shut up. But that didn't stop her. She's fucking evil."

"What the hell happened to you?" Nadia asked again.

"You!" he shouted. "Her!" he wiped his mouth again. "You happened to me! But I found what worked. It numbs me so much I don't care what she does or how much she cuts me. Another finger. Oh my! I can't even feel it." He looked at his hand. "Another thumb! Oh, please Cassy, not my thumb! Please, not my thumb!" He started laughing again.

"Foskett!" Nadia shouted. "I need to talk to you!"

"What the hell is this?" a voice demanded. They both turned as an S-O levelled his rifle at them. Another climbed out of the humvee parked in front of their doorway. "I said, what is this? Get your hands where I can see them, both of you, and get down here slowly!" Nadia stepped out of the doorway. Foskett shed his blanket and joined her, squinting in the sunlight.

"Some junkie and his whore," the second S-O said. He raised his rifle.

"No, no, no, we're just talking. It's cool," Foskett said.

He took a step forward with his hands open and stumbled. There were three sharp cracks, Foskett flew backwards and slumped in the doorway. His shirt began to turn red. Nadia screamed until a gloved hand hit her mouth.

"Shut the fuck up, you little whore!" An S-O reached out and grabbed her dress. He pulled hard and it ripped down the front, exposing her breasts. "Looking for tricks after curfew and you wonder what happens?" He grabbed her roughly and squeezed her ass. "Tricks for free now, huh?"

"Just end her and let's go," commanded the other.

"Dad," Nadia said.

"Dad," she said again.

"Dad!" she said louder.

"Who the fuck is she calling? Shut the bitch up and let's get the fuck out of here!"

Nadia watched as the S-O pointed his rifle at her. She heard a loud sound and felt a tearing at her chest. Her world went black.

Nadia came out of her trance screaming and clutching her chest. She saw Foskett sitting in front of her. When he was close enough, she hit him across the face with her fist. Nadia bent over and retched until she vomited on the carpet. She covered her face and sobbed.

"Nadia, what happened?" Foskett asked when her tears slowed.

"I got shot! That's what happened you son of bitch!"

"Did I ... ?"

"Yes, you got shot too. You lied to me! You've been lying the whole time!" Nadia said.

"I don't know what you're talking about, Nadia. What happened?" Foskett said.

"She's in your head! She's been in your head the whole time, ever since I had to come here. You've been acting like I was the crazy one. Where are they? Where are they, huh?" Nadia rose and walked toward Foskett's desk.

"Where are what, Nadia?" Now Foskett was on his feet too.

"Your drugs, Foskett. The drugs you take to try to block her out. Are they in here?" Nadia reached down and pulled at a desk drawer. It was locked.

"Nadia, calm down. Tell me what happened," Foskett said.

"Don't you tell me to calm down, you junkie. You know everything I've told you is true. Everything. And you still give me my fucking meds and make me sit here every week," Nadia sat at Foskett's desk, slumped in exhaustion.

Foskett sat down on the couch Nadia had just vacated.

"Why did you lie?" Nadia asked. "Why did you just pretend nothing was happening?"

Foskett put his head in his hands. "What could I do? Do you think I could admit that there is some presence controlling you through your dreams, that that presence is torturing me in mine? What do you think would happen, Nadia? What do you seriously think they would do to the both of us?"

"You could have told me. Maybe—"

"Maybe what? Maybe I just told you. Now what do we do? I can't get away from her, Nadia. I can't ... she ..." Foskett fell silent.

Nadia watched her counsellor from the desk. She kicked the locked drawers. "What have you got in here, anyway?" she asked. "It's gotta be some really good shit from the way you looked."

"Nadia, you have to tell me what happened. You went under, and then you went silent. Your eyes were moving under your lids, so I knew you were—"

"I found you in a doorway drugged out of your head, that's what happened!" Nadia said. "You said she was in your head from the moment you met me, that you took anything you could to stop her, but nothing worked. What the hell is going on?"

"I don't know!" Foskett cried. "Fuck! This is too fucked up. I told them I didn't want you, that I had too much already, that—"

"Pull yourself together, you dick!" Nadia shouted.

He looked at Nadia. "What do we do now?" he asked.

"I need time," she said. "And I need you off my back." She looked at the desk, at the yellow pad with Foskett's scribbles. "I need some notes. Write me some notes so I can be late to school. With no dates or times this time!" Nadia glanced around the room. "I don't know. Write your reports and shit, but keep me away from the cops."

Foskett stared at Nadia, nodding. "I can do that," he said. He picked Nadia's bag off the floor and opened it. He reached in and took out her bottle of meds. He opened the bottle and shook out a white pill.

"Do you mind if I have a mint?" he asked.

"How'd you know?" she answered.

"Don't you think I've tried that stuff? They make you comatose. You end up not caring if she cuts you. You even laugh when she does it. That really pisses her off." He giggled nervously. "So, it was pretty obvious you weren't taking your pills."

"Help yourself," Nadia said.

N adia waited by the 79th Street station. She sat at the same bench she had the two previous mornings, before giving up and using Foskett's note to get into school late. Additional sessions, therapeutic exercises, she didn't care what he'd written, just as long as his signature and stamp was at the bottom. He had signed a week's worth and promised more at her next session.

Jakob emerged from an ally across the street. Nadia followed him with her eyes as he approached the bench and sat next to her. His hair was tied in the back. He wore an old green sweater with a few holes and black denim jeans. Just another hipster. Maybe a musician. He wouldn't look so out of place if he were in a different part of town.

"What took you so long?" Nadia asked. Jakob turned his face towards hers and raised an eyebrow.

"Anyway, you're here, like I hoped," she said.

"You look tired," Jakob said.

"Yeah, well, sleep just hasn't been that restful. We need to talk. Let's find somewhere quieter." Nadia stood and started to walk away.

"I know what she wants," she added.

Jakob followed as she walked away from the station. She tried to retrace the route they had taken before. Jakob tapped her on the shoulder and pointed when he thought she was taking a wrong turn.

She finally stopped in front of a burned-out building. A charred sign advertised Jamaican Jerk Chicken.

"It looks closed," Jakob said.

Nadia walked to a nearby bus stop. "What happened to Frank's?" she asked a man waiting.

"Burned down," he said.

"Oh, *really*?"

"You friends with Frank?" he asked.

"Only met him once," Nadia said. "We were just after some chicken."

"Right," he said as he looked her over. He glanced at Jakob. "Folks say NLM torched the joint. Say they heard Frank shouting, then just heard quiet. S-O found his charred remains. That's what happens to narks."

He looked away from Nadia and in the direction of the expected bus. Nadia walked back past Jakob. He followed her as she made her way back along 79th and continued west, away from the station. The number of storefronts increased as they walked. Dollar shops, check cashing loan traps, cleaners, beauticians, budget grocery. A garish blue sign seemed to act like a beacon. Nadia stopped in front of a small Mexican cafe.

"This looks safe," she said. "Neutral, at least." She entered and sat at a booth. Jakob sat across from her. He began to speak but she held up a finger. A waitress came over with two glasses of water and menus. Nadia glanced quickly at one.

"*Dos enchilada suizas, por favor,*" she said.

"You'll like that. I think," she said to Jakob as the waitress left.

"Thank you. How have you been?" he asked.

Nadia opened her mouth to speak but nothing came out. She shook her head.

"You said you know what she wants," Jakob said.

"Yeah, that's right. She wants us to make sure a man gets elected, or chosen to be elected. The guy who became the President after Roosevelt died. He actually did become President. We're to help it happen, I guess."

"And?"

"That's it. Make sure it happens. Make sure he gets nominated as the Vice President during the party convention. Help the good guy win, like he did, like he was supposed to."

"Helping good guys win doesn't sound too much like your Miss Beil," Jakob said.

"No, it doesn't." Nadia looked Jakob in the eyes as she spoke.

"But it must be pivotal, important, maybe, in a way we can't see right now. Is that why you called me?" he asked.

"Called you? What do you mean?"

"You wanted me to come. You waited for me. And here I am."

"I don't know what you mean. I knew you would show up. I—"

Jakob smiled. "You used intention. You may not have been aware of it, but you did. It's very powerful when it's focused. It's a tool. It allows you to go anywhere in your dreams," he said.

"I still don't know why you're here. Why do you care, even? Why should I trust you?"

"I ... I asked, in a way. I realize that sounds odd. But that is what I did. I've spent a lot of time trying to harness my dreams, or what I ... what we can do in our dreams. I travelled a lot of those lines I was talking about before—"

"Your tree branches?"

"A tree is just one way to describe it. During the day I write books and stories about those travels. 'Alternate Travel' is a genre I seemed to have started. Descriptions and guides to other realities. People like the stories and I sell lots of books. But that started to feel ... I don't know. It started to feel like I was being selfish. Wasting my potential. So, I started to go into sleep with an intention, like learning more about dreaming. Or a simple one: where should I be now? Where am I needed? One night I opened my eyes and saw the L and sat next to you. Turns out I was needed after all, doesn't it?" Jakob said.

"I dreamed the future," she said. "It wasn't very nice. Can you do that?"

"If the intention is to see what might be, then yes, I can. What we see is potential. Why did you dream forward?" Jakob asked.

"My therapist hypnotized me. He ... he didn't really know what he was doing, but it worked. I found him. And I got killed. I thought you couldn't die in dreams."

"You can feel pain, you know that. So why wouldn't you be able to die? But dying merely closes a window. It means you can never go back to that place."

"Thank God for that," Nadia said. "Well ... you know what I mean."

The waitress brought two plates and set them down. She looked at Nadia and frowned. Nadia noticed the crucifix around the woman's neck. Jakob took a bite of the food.

"Much spicier than where I am from. It's almost Azteca, just milder," he said.

"Yeah," Nadia said. "We're in a Mexican restaurant."

"She must really value you. And maybe fear you," Jakob said. "Has she told you anything specific about why you are there?"

"She said it was my skin, and my skills," Nadia answered.

"Skills?"

"Skills, she calls them," Nadia said. "Like putting a finger through a desk. I can do that when I am in that classroom. Or walking through a wall. She had me do that again and again. Why are you grinning at me?"

"That's called Dream Yoga, Nadia. Monks train for years to be able to do that. Sounds like you do it naturally. No wonder she's trying to control you, but when you realize what you can do without her, she'll—"

"You sound like the other guy now," Nadia said.

"Other guy? Who are you talking about?" Jakob asked.

"The other guy, tweed suit and a bad haircut. He's been following me and Randall and June. He tried to talk to me about her," she said. "He wasn't from there, at least that's what it felt like. Like he didn't belong. Like me. What's the matter? You know him?"

Jakob glanced out the window, though he was certain he wouldn't see anybody. "I don't know," he said. "Somebody tried to kill me once. But not in a dream, when I was awake. But he was dreaming. Bad haircut ... Did he have blue eyes?" Jakob asked.

"Shit, I can't remember. I don't even think I looked. I was more interested in how to get away."

"Good. I mean, be careful."

"If he killed you when you weren't dreaming ...?"

"I wouldn't wake up. All I could do was make sure he couldn't try to kill me again," Jakob said.

"What does that mean? Are you saying somebody can come from a dream and murder me here?" Nadia asked.

"That's one thing I've been trying to tell you. What do you think Miss Beil meant when she told you about assassinations or babies dying? What I meant when I told you to be careful?" Jakob asked.

"I had just knifed a guy," Nadia hissed more than whispered. "I wasn't catching every word you were saying!"

"OK. So now you know. I'm here, so others could be here. Like this guy with the hair. In my reality somebody tried to kill me, and it may have been him. If he killed me when I was awake, I would be dead. Really dead. Just like if you get killed when you're awake. You keep safe, watch out for ... people who don't seem to belong and for the time being do as Miss Beil says. Try to learn as much as you can." Jakob finished the last of his enchilada and wiped his mouth on a napkin. He looked around the cafe, then outside the windows again. "I'm going to go now. The next time I see you might be earlier," he said. "Earlier in time. I want to see this place you are going to."

"You'll have to do something about that hair then," Nadia said. "Hey," she added. "I still don't know why I should trust you."

"Like you said, what choice do you have?" Jakob reached over and placed his hand over hers. He squeezed it gently, removed his hand and stood.

"Jakob," Nadia started, then gazed at her plate. "I'm trapped. Here or when I sleep. I can't see any way out. Help me get out," she said.

"It can get really lonely. I know what it's like. I've been there," he said. "But now you're not alone. Remember that."

Jakob reclined on his bed and closed his eyes. He rested his head on a high pillow. His legs were loosely crossed. The sleep he sought was light, too much comfort would be too difficult to wake in. He rested his hands on his stomach, one on top of the other, not out of any ritual purpose, but sheer habit. He focused his intention, bringing a question to mind and keeping it there.

Jakob calmed his breathing, relaxing into a soft pattern of inhalation and exhalation. When his mind was clear he focused his attention on the crown of his head. There he saw luminous white light, which he entered. After several minutes his attention travelled down to his throat. There he visualized a beautiful red lotus with four petals. He studied the fold of each petal. In the center a crystal made of pure light.

When he was confident of his concentration, Jakob took his attention down into his heart. His heart was a twelve petalled green lotus. All the petals surrounded a central field, in which sat a sound in the form of a syllable from the Tibetan language. At the top sat the *tig-lé*, the drop, the point of consciousness. This rested in a half moon. Underneath was the letter *Ha*, a seed syllable linking all sounds; it was a doorway. Below this sat the letter '*a*', the first of all sounds, symbolizing infinite space. Beneath that was the vowel mark, a curl resembling a question mark on its side. He studied each detail in the form of *Hung*, the heart syllable.

At first, he had struggled with this technique when he first learned it on a visit to the Tibetan monastery in Herefordshire, the first monastery established in the Norse world. The Buddhist kingdom was becoming the center of spirituality in a world of many gods, offering a way for all to live in harmony. Tibetans believed they were not only living at the roof of the world, but that they were a light in the darkness. The Great Opening initiated by the Fourteenth Dalai Lama continued to thrive. Embassies and monasteries were even opening in the Islamic Republics.

As he developed the skill, Jakob would travel to the kingdom itself, and in his dreams sit with past or present Tibetan masters, practicing, always practicing. He sat below Jigmed Lingpa in his mountain monastery. He practiced with Dzogchen Rinpoches. Most greeted him with laughter when he first asked for teaching, as if expecting the fair skinned visitor, but they shared their dharma.

Jakob laid on his bed with his eyes closed, focusing all of his concentration and attention, devoid of all thought, except an intention.

When he felt ready Jakob visualized thousands of blue *Hungs* coming from both nostrils with each exhalation. They originated in his heart, travelled up and left through his nostrils with his breath. As they spread out, they illuminated all space. He inhaled and the light of the *hungs* returned, illuminating and dissolving his body and mind. He dissolved into the light. He breathed in and out twenty-one times, just as he was taught.

"Who is Cassy Beil?" he silently asked.

He intuitively felt something wrong with the question and tried again.

"What is Cassy Beil?" he asked.

Jakob felt his body sink deeper. He felt a calming darkness blanket his body, cover his mind. He maintained focus on the lotus, on the letter, but they were fading, growing dimmer.

Jakob opened his eyes to a world of blinding white cold. Ahead was a frozen sea, sculpted by ceaseless winds. Great slabs of ice were thrust up creating an impassable barrier. Snow blew in drifts, swirling past his feet and ankles, building up against his legs. He was slowly being buried.

Jakob lifted a leg free and took a step forward. He pulled the other leg out and moved it forward too, but by this time, the first was almost buried again.

"Which of the Nine Realms am I in?" he thought. *Helheim,* home of the dead who did not die bravely and who were not brave enough to go to *Valhalla,* who would never feel joy or happiness again? *Niflheim,* a world of fog and mist, the first of the Nine Worlds, the darkest and coldest region?

"Am I seeing *Elivagar,* the ice waves, in the distance?" he thought.

He shook his legs free again, a much more difficult task, and stepped forward. He was confused and disoriented. This was not a world he knew. This was not a place where humans dwelt, no reality created by them, or their 'gods'.

Jakob heard a crunching sound, snow and ice being compacted underfoot. Then another, and another. He peered into the swirling snow where movement caught his eye. A great shape with a beard of ice on a grimacing face came towards him, emerging from the dim. On its head was a helmet—twisted, knotted horns emerged through it from the massive skull. Its freezing breath blew onto Jakob's face as it came closer. Its skin was as blue as glacial ice, eyes a menacing obsidian glare. It wore ragged fur around its waist, thick brown pelts ripped from a mammoth's flank. In its hand it held a huge double headed axe, each blade a slab of razor-sharp ice.

Jakob tried to raise his leg but couldn't. His feet were frozen to the ground, his legs buried in drift. He realized what was upon him, but he didn't understand why, couldn't grasp what he was seeing. A *jötunn*? A frost giant? Jakob had travelled to many realities, but never to these realms, places of myth and story. Surely, they were not real? *Ice giants are a cultural image*, he thought, only with intuition. *A cultural image is an illusion, a guise. It is used by our minds to comprehend, and used by the gods to take form.*

The beast raised its axe, ready to swing.

Jakob closed his eyes. He let go of all fear, all thought, and sunk into the blackness of his mind. He drifted in the bardo, the place between worlds, between existences. He dreamed within his dream, and went even deeper.

"*What* is Cassy Beil?" he asked in the darkness.

J akob opened his eyes and immediately raised his arm to shield them. A bright red glare filled the sky. His senses were assaulted by sound and smell. Screams filled the air, rancid with the scent of excrement and decay. He slowly lowered his arm, letting his eyes adjust to what was both bright and also gloom.

He looked to the left and saw a desert of burning sand. Naked people were struggling to walk up a dune as the skin on their feet blistered and oozed with pus. Skin flaked from their feet, until bones were visible, yet they continued upward. Some fell to their knees, and smoke rose from where they knelt. Some struggled to rise and fell, writhing in agony as their skin turned red, blistered, and blackened in the heat. Others rose and continued on bone stumps.

To the right, wild dogs were chasing people. He watched as they sank their teeth into the people, jaws tearing and ripping off hunks of flesh. Screams filled the air. Winged creatures descended into the panicked crowd, gripping their victims in razor sharp talons. Their beaks flashed and a hunk of cheek disappeared, revealing teeth and jaw bone. A flick of a beast's head and a man reeled back clutching where his eye had been.

Jakob surveyed the surrounding area. On one hill, feet and legs protruded where bodies had been buried head first. Some were still moving, feet kicking in vain. Directly in front of him lay a pit with steep banks. Within the pit people tried to claw their way to the surface, their hands bloodied as their nails tore off. The sides of the pit were studded with finger nails. Horned, spider like creatures moved among the people, with flashing blades and hooks in each of their arms. Jakob saw a flash of metal and one of the humans collapsed in two parts. A creature quickly pounced, burying its face in the opened torso.

A hook flew through the air and embedded in the back of a fleeing woman. She was pulled backwards, arms wheeling for purchase. The creature sunk its teeth into her neck, covering itself in blood. The creatures seemed to be grinning, but only because they had no lips. In one corner of the pit Jakob saw a man tied to a cross being flayed alive. Each strip of skin was devoured before the creature continued with the next incision.

Through a sulfurous mist he felt a presence approach. The glint of tarnished armor caught his eye, a chest plate scratched and dented. Wings rose from its back, made of feathers that were grey with age and dirt. The expression on its face was pure malice. Red eyes stared at him through the gloom. Behind it were more like itself, overseeing the macabre spectacle around him.

He knew it was who he was looking for. Cassy Beil in her—its—true form.

Before he could react, a hook flew towards him and embedded itself in the flesh of his chest. He instinctively leaned back, wincing as the hook pulled at his muscle. Without thinking he grabbed the hook and pulled it out. Blood ran out of the deep wound left behind. He looked up and saw another hook fly towards him and embed itself into the flesh of his thigh. He staggered back and the hook tore lose, taking flesh with it. Before regaining his balance, he was struck again. His shoulder exploded in pain and he was jerked forward. Another hook bit into his side.

Jakob repeated a mantra, taught by Tibetan monks to prepare for death, for navigating the bardo, the space between life and the next incarnation.

I will abandon all thoughts of fear and terror, I will recognize whatever appears as my projection.

I will abandon all thoughts of fear and terror, I will recognize whatever appears as my projection.

I will abandon all thoughts of fear and terror, I will recognize whatever appears as my projection.

"A cultural image is an illusion, a guise. It is used by our minds to comprehend, and used by the gods to take form," he repeated.

And yet the hooks continued to land and embed in his skin, pulling him nearer the beast with red eyes. It might be a cultural image, Jakob started to realize, but it had a reality of its own, an illusion given power by the cultural belief in it.

Jakob felt a presence behind him, a warm breath in his ear. He heard a familiar voice. He knew who it was and he was relieved.

"Leave, Jakob. You do not know the danger you are in," Artemis said.

Jakob stared ahead as the red eyed creature neared. He felt the hooks pull the flesh away from his bones. Pain began to overwhelm him.

"Leave, Jakob. Now!" she insisted. It was not a request, but an order.

Jakob closed his eyes. He let go of all fear, all thought, and sunk into the blackness of his mind. He felt the hooks loosen their grip, then he lost all physical sensation. He fell into nothingness.

Jakob woke drenched in sweat. His heart beat furiously, threatening to explode in his chest. He gasped, caught his breath, and gasped again.

The light of dawn began to illuminate his room. He felt the smooth, unopened skin of his chest and legs, and lay in bed until his breathing steadied and his heart slowed. Putting his feet on the floor he slowly sat up and cradled his head in his hands. "You do not know the danger you are in," she had said. And he *didn't* know, he had no idea. Dying in a dream meant waking up. It meant a reality closed.

This felt very different.

Jakob rose and walked to the window, a large span of glass panes offering a view of the city. The London skyline spread before him. His reality. His time and place. Roof gardens added green to an otherwise grey scene. Arrays of solar panels reflected the early sun on south facing walls. The Thames flowed slowly on its way to the *Nordsea*. Airships hung majestically on their moorings high above the streets, their comfortable gondolas suspended beneath the long cylindrical bodies. They were the main reason he had taken this apartment—watching these long ships of the air rise and gently move away, to the capital, Yorvik, or much farther. Across the Western Ocean to the far settlements. Iceland, Greenland, Markland, even to New Yorvik itself, the gateway to the New World.

He glanced at a faded picture on the shelf, a series of small photos on a strip of card, typical of tourist booths found in the city. The photo was purposefully positioned close to the window, framed by sky and airships. A woman smiled. She was holding a small boy. He could see the sadness in his mother's eyes. It was the last time he had seen his mother, before she crossed the ocean to start a new life. He had been supposed to follow later. Only her airship had never reached its destination, lost in a storm over the Western Ocean.

On the wall behind the photo strip was a framed book cover draft of his first 'novel', as other people called it, and part of the reason why he could afford his view over the Thames. The illustration showed a young man leading three Viking warriors through the forest, in search of royal game. In the youth's hand was a knife, not yet bloodied. Jakob had wanted that removed from the image, but his editor had had the final say. Unaware of it at the time, Artemis guided him the entire way, ensuring this present would come to pass. She watched unseen when the prey was cornered and he did what was required.

At the moment Jakob felt only confusion. There was much to process. But it would be a long day, with lots of time to think before dreaming again.

His father, the other reason he stayed in the city, would soon be waiting at the coffee house. He dressed quickly and made his way to the street.

Nadia smiled as she approached the school's entrance. She enjoyed arriving by herself, after the crowds of students had already passed through the bag checks and metal detectors. She touched her face. It was the first time she had smiled in quite a while. Her step was light as she opened the first set of doors.

Nadia gave the black clad school security guard Foskett's note and passed through the metal detectors. A guard rifled through her bag. "Anything I might cut my hand on in here?" he asked. He turned the bag upside down and spilled all the contents on the table. He poked through her belongings with a pen.

The other guard handed back her note. "Must be nice just doin' your own thing, huh?" he asked.

"I was at therapy. The note—"

"Sure you were. Of course you were," he said.

"How much can you get for these from the miscreants that go to this school?" the guard asked. Nadia's pills were in his hand. "I bet they go down real nice, make the world a pretty place for you, am I right?" He pried off the top and sniffed. "Smells alright. How about you share them wit' us?"

"They're my prescription," Nadia said. "My psych—"

"Yeah, save it for your teachers," the guard said. He turned the bottle upside down, emptying the contents on the table. "Clean up your mess and get to class."

The guard pointed to his head and twirled his finger. Nadia refilled her medicine bottle, picked up her bag and scooped her belongings into it. She walked carefully down the hall without looking back.

Mr. Johnson was in his stride as Nadia entered class. His cheeks were flushed and a small speck of saliva sat at the corner of his mouth. He stopped speaking and watched her enter. Nadia ignored him, turning immediately to the flag and putting her hand over her heart.

"Eenie meenie miney moe, catch a nigger by the toe," she mouthed silently. "If he hollers let him go, eenie meenie miney moe."

She smiled at the flag, then at Mr. Johnson. "I'm sorry, Mr. Johnson. I have a note," she said. She placed it on his desk before taking her own seat.

Mr. Johnson glanced at the note but decided to ignore it. He watched Nadia sit down and look up at him. "We were discussing respect, Nadia, quite appropriately. But specifically, respect for ...?" He looked around the room and chose a face with the longest scowl. He pointed. "You."

"Respect for the uniform, sir," she said.

"Exactly. We have uniforms for a reason. They set apart those who choose to serve society, and as a result deserve our respect," he looked at Nadia. "The police are an example, putting their lives on the line so that our streets can be safe. We can feel safe, because we have those brave men in uniform patrolling our streets and manning our checkpoints." His eyes did not leave Nadia, who was staring back at her teacher. He could see by the movement in her temples that he was getting through. She was biting hard enough to crack a nut.

"They keep our streets free from criminals and radicals who would ..." Mr. Johnson let the words float around his student who had arrived, yet again, with a free pass to flaunt at him.

"And there are other uniforms, those worn by the brave men and women who defend this nation by serving in the armed forces. The Navy. The Air Force. The Army. The Marines. Respect for the uniform is an acknowledgement of the sacrifice these fine people make to protect our democracy and way of life."

Nadia raised her hand slowly, realizing that it was already too late for her to leave class unscathed. Maybe Foskett could get her assigned to another school, even home study. Maybe this was her chance ...

"Yes, Nadia?" Mr. Johnson asked.

"Those police you talk about? They kill whoever they want and never get stopped. Keeping us all free in the land of the free. You know your S-O rape girls in their Humvees, don't you? You respect them for that? You know some of those girls are even in this room." Nadia looked directly at a girl in the second row who was staring at her desktop. Linda, was that her name? She saw Mr. Johnson clench a fist and then release it.

"Killers and rapists," she said. "So salute their uniform."

"And I was wondering," Nadia found she couldn't stop herself. "These fine people in the Navy, with their sharp blue uniforms. When was the last time they actually fought an enemy that had a navy, Mr. Johnson? I mean, like the Air Force. Has the US Air Force ever fought a country with an air force of its own? After Germany and Japan. Which was a *long* time ago."

"What is it that you are trying to say, Nadia? Are you saying that—"

"I think I'm saying that you want us to respect the uniform of police that kill us and rape us, and get a hard on every time we see an army uniform, an army that never fights anybody that can *actually* fight back." She saw it on the news many times. Another intervention. Another drone attack. Another story about protecting American freedoms.

Nadia watched her teacher's face grow darker. She felt the eyes of her classmates on her. "I mean, dropping the atom bomb on Hanoi killed hundreds of thousands of people like you and me."

"Communists are not like me, young lady!" Mr. Johnson could feel his face flush, feel his cheeks start to tingle. He was getting angry, not just pretending to be mad to make a point. Nadia had started to invade his dreams, strange, uncomfortable dreams that fled his memory as soon he woke, leaving only a feeling of foreboding. Mr. Johnson knew there were other ways to manipulate the children in front of him. Students are adept at locating and pressing a teacher's button, but more potent is a teacher's ability to maneuver students to do what they want, pushing them far enough to hang themselves with the rope offered. *Here Nadia, have some more rope,* Mr. Johnson thought. *And get the hell out of my life.*

"Brave men and women in uniform, keeping us safe from poor Afghan farmers or Cuban peasants," Nadia went on.

"Nadia, I think we've heard enough," he said, and smiled. "You've certainly given us a lot to think about."

"Just shut up, girl," a large girl whispered beside her.

"Nadia has given me an excellent idea for homework," Mr. Johnson said. He smiled as he heard groans. "Each and every one of you will write a six-page essay on why we should respect the uniform of those who serve so that we can live free. In fact, that will be the title. Write that down now. Then Miss Ifedi, whom you can thank, will remove herself from this classroom!"

Students sullenly opened notebooks to a fresh sheet of paper.

Nadia did as she was told. She wrote the title on a piece of paper, ripped it out of her notebook, took it to Mr. Johnson's desk and slammed it down. She turned and was met by the glares of her classmates. She walked to the door, slowing only to pick up her bag, and was it not for the hydraulic hinge of the door would have heard a satisfying slam behind her. Instead she heard Mr. Johnson crumple a piece a paper.

"Don't worry, class," he said. "She has a note."

Nadia heard laughter in the room.

Nadia walked to the empty cafeteria. She slowed her breathing and tried to slow her mind. She felt like the day was a live hand grenade and she had just pulled the pin. She tried to remember how she felt before reaching school. Almost hopeful. Not so alone.

Nadia watched the cafeteria staff putting out trays of food under the heat lamps. She walked to the counter and picked up a plate. The smell of cheese brought her to a pan of pizza slices and she took two. She added a scoop of French fries. She couldn't remember ever eating them warm. A woman with a blue apron came out and stood waiting by the cash register. "You're too early," she started to say.

Nadia ignored her and sat at a table. The hall was eerily quiet. She picked up her pizza and took a bite, putting off the moment when she would have to think about what she had done. Nadia was saved from further thinking by a loud bell sounding the end of a period and the beginning of the first lunch rotation. Students began filing into the cafeteria, plates clattered, chairs scraped. Nadia's shoulder was jostled as somebody sat next to her. Linda. The girl who was raped at the checkpoint. Another classmate sat across from Nadia, and she could feel somebody behind her.

"What the fuck is the matter with you?" the girl across from her asked. "You open your mouth and we get extra work."

"Johnson's an asshole," Nadia said.

"Who the fuck cares? All you have to do is keep your mouth shut," the girl said from across the table. "You can't even do that."

"I didn't say anything that most people don't already think," Nadia said.

"Fuck that NLM shit. They're just another gang of thugs no better than the S-O," Linda said.

Nadia looked over at Linda. "How can you say that? After what they did to you in their Humvee?"

"Fuck you," the Linda said. The girl behind Nadia reached over and picked up a French fry. She studied it for a moment before dropping it into Nadia's lap.

"Fucking bitch with attitude, thinks nobody cares," the student behind Nadia said. "Thinks she knows what happens. She don't know shit, but she talk talk talk in every class."

"Johnson practically gave us permission to help with your learning. You're going to take a beaten' now."

Nadia tried to stand but the student behind shoved her back down. She turned towards Linda to speak but gasped as Linda hit her in the stomach. "Fucking bitch, you don't know nothin'. Crazy piece of shit," she said as she punched Nadia again.

Nadia was pulled backwards and fell off her chair. She quickly scrambled to her feet. Others had risen as quickly to watch the show and Nadia was soon surrounded by students eager to watch. Her three classmates knew they only had a moment and didn't waste time. Linda grabbed a handful of hair as another hit Nadia in the face. Nadia regained her feet and stumbled towards the table, reaching out to steady herself. Her hand hit a utensil and she grabbed it. She spun with it in her hand and felt it connect with something soft. She heard a scream.

The circle around her widened and she saw Linda holding her leg. Nadia looked at her empty hand, then again at Linda's leg. Her denim jeans were turning red where the knife stuck out. Linda looked at Nadia wide eyed, momentarily confused. They both looked at the piece of metal in the girl's leg.

"Crazy bitch," she heard.

Two men in black came closer and the students quickly moved out of their way. "Knife!" she heard one shout. He reached into his holster, pulled out something black and pointed it at her. A dart stabbed into her chest and she screamed as 50,000 volts surged through her body. She lost control and collapsed to the floor. The other guard approached, pulled out his electric prod and touched it to her already quivering body. Her muscles spasmed as he prodded again. A guard stood on her hand and kicked her in the head. Nadia didn't see anything at all after that.

36

F oskett found Nadia on Unit 7, strapped to a gurney. He gently touched the purple bruise covering half her face. He lifted her gown and counted five burns left by the cattle prod. He started unstrapping her arms and legs. He had studied her medication chart. She was too doped up on Haldol to know what was happening, and he didn't have much time. The release papers he had forged wouldn't pass a closer inspection, and he was sure those papers would be examined in more detail. A medical release of a violent psychopath to the care of her therapist? A live prisoner leaving the unit? They usually didn't leave that way. Nadia managed once, but it was very slim odds she would twice. Luckily, actual thinking was above the paygrade of the officer on duty and he accepted Foskett's story.

Foskett half lifted, half dragged Nadia to a waiting wheelchair. He felt a muscle pull as he wrestled her into a sitting position. He pushed her into the hall and headed for the entrance. He didn't get twenty paces before he was stopped.

"Hey, doc, hold on there a moment," the officer said. The police man was scanning the release form, peering as if he had forgotten his reading glasses or struggling with words that were too big. Foskett's hands became slippery on the chair handles. He wiped his palms on his pants.

"There's gotta be a place you have to sign. Don't seem right you can just wheel a prisoner away," the officer said.

"No," Foskett said. "That wouldn't be right at all. Here." Foskett decided the fewer words spoken the better. He walked to the desk and picked up the form, pretended to search for a line, reached for a pen and signed the bottom.

"There you go," he tried to say calmly. He returned to Nadia and pushed the chair away from the officer, out of the door, and quickly across the parking lot. Getting Nadia into his car was another awkward wrestling match. He pushed the empty chair away from the car and jumped behind the wheel. He checked the rear-view mirror, expecting officers to rush out, but the night was quiet.

Foskett drove out of the car park and made his way to the expressway. He rolled down his window and with the flick of a wrist his cell phone sailed out. *So that is what a burning bridge looks like*, he thought. *A thin plastic rectangle flying past my peripheral vision.* He travelled a familiar route, taken many times while his mother was alive. Her two-bedroom house on the westside was still there. His plans to renovate it, maybe even move in, were always delayed by the amount of work it would actually take. The run-down cottage was now the only hiding place he could think of. No phone, no internet, utilities still in his mother's name. It might work for a few days.

He turned off the busy expressway onto a dimly lit street. At the detached garage he pressed the door opener clipped to his visor, grateful that it still worked. The door opened to offer a welcome sanctuary. He relaxed once the door closed behind him. He sat in the darkness staring ahead for several moments. Looking over at the slumped figure next to him he sighed. One more gauntlet to run before they were home.

Foskett left the car and opened the back door to the garage. The neighbors' lights were off and their houses were quiet. He walked down the path and unlocked the back door to the house, leaving the door slightly ajar. Returning to his car he opened the passenger door and lifted Nadia out. He tried to hoist her to his shoulder but her limp form made it impossible. Leaning her against the car he tried instead to carry her in his arms. He made it to the path before needing to rest. He listened for any noise from the neighbors and struggled to the house in silence. He pushed open the back door with a foot, pulled Nadia inside, sat her in the doorway leading to the kitchen and closed and locked the house door.

He carried Nadia through the kitchen and into the first bedroom. The small room had a bed in the middle with just enough space to walk around. He pulled back the covers, readied the waiting saline solution and arranged a selection of drugs. Moving Nadia into the bed involved grasping her under her shoulders, climbing onto the bed and dragging her behind him. Dropping her upper body on the bed he hoisted her feet up and pushed her sideways until she was in the middle. He covered her with a sheet and sat down beside her.

Foskett looked at the drugged and unconscious girl lying beside him. Her face was bruised and swollen but peaceful. There was no tension, no eye movement under her lids. She wasn't dreaming, he hoped. He wondered what peaceful might look like on *his* face. Freedom from that creature in his nightmares.

He got off the bed and walked around the house. It didn't take long. The bedroom was right off the open plan lounge and dining room. He walked past the small dining table and was soon standing in front of the two-seater sofa. A 'love seat', he remembered it being called. Its size required you to sit close to the person next to you. The sofa faced the opposite wall, where an old radio sat. No TV, no internet, no instant traces.

Foskett tried the front door. It was still locked. He checked the piece of clear tape stuck to the frame. It was unbroken. He felt silly. He saw that on an old movie he watched when he was twelve. Caution was necessary now. The door was part of the house since it was built almost a hundred years before. It was seldom used. Even when he was a boy, they always used the back. A knock on the front door meant a stranger or a salesman. Usually it was Christ for sale, pictured in some paradise like setting. Green fields, people petting lions, deer grazing nearby.

"Would you like to live in a place like this?" he remembered a stranger asking his mother.

"I already do," she replied.

Foskett opened the door onto the front porch. It slanted down at an odd angle. Two window panes were already cracked, more threatened to break as the porch continued its slide downward under rotting footings that he would have to repair. They were another reason for putting off repairs to the place. He knew little about foundations.

He returned to the lounge and opened the door to the second bedroom. The single pull out bed would do for the foreseeable future. His mother had bought it at a store selling used hotel furniture years before so he would have a place to sleep when he stayed over. He did that increasingly as she became older and needed him more. It was too small and incredibly uncomfortable. When folded away it became an oversized chair allowing his mother the pretense of living in a bigger house.

Foskett walked through the Jack and Jill that connected the two bedrooms. The room was the length of the tub, which was not even long enough to straighten your legs in. He closed his door and opened the one leading into where Nadia lay. He sat next to her on the bed again. It was time to bring her out of her drugged haze. He hoped he could do it, and he hoped she would agree with his plan.

37

Haloperidol injected into muscle has a long-lasting effect. The amount administered to Nadia at the station's psych ward meant she wouldn't regain full control of her muscles for several days, regardless of what Foskett did to revive her. It was possible that she would never recover. Most 'patients' in custody die from overdose. Had he not arrived, her next dose could have killed her.

Foskett rummaged through his bag of tricks. There is no such thing as a failed med student, he had once heard, only an intelligent user. And every drug has a reversal, as long you don't take too much. He took Nadia's arm and straightened it. He ran his fingers over the soft flesh. She had good veins. He thought he would have made a good doctor, maybe in a different time or place. He filled a syringe with Flumazenil, tapped out any air, and inserted the needle. It wasn't the best drug, but it was all he could steal in the limited time he had had. Good Flumazenil is always handy to have ready in case of an overdose.

He pushed down on the syringe and watched the clear fluid disappear into her vein. He removed the needle and waited. Nadia remained still and peaceful and he relaxed. Then her hand began to shake and soon the rest of her body followed. He jumped up and stood with his back against the wall a mere two feet from her spasming body. He had expected this response but hoped it would be less violent than what he saw. The bed darkened beneath her as she lost control of her bladder. He pushed her over to her side and let her convulse. Just when he thought they wouldn't, the spasms started to slow. Finally, they stopped. He heard a gasp, followed by deep breathes.

"What!" Nadia gasped.

Foskett rolled her onto her back and tried to reassure her. "It's OK, you're safe now."

Nadia tried to get up but her body wouldn't cooperate. "Get off me! Let me go!" she rasped. She tried to rise once more but gave up.

"Nadia, you're safe now. Relax. You're OK," he said. "You're OK."

"What's going on?" she asked. She groaned. "I hurt. Everywhere."

"Just try to relax. You're safe now. We're safe now."

"Foskett?" she asked. "Why's everything blurry?"

"It's a side effect. It'll clear. I took you from the police and brought you to my mother's," Foskett said.

"Where's your mother?" Nadia's voice slurred.

"She's dead," Foskett said.

Nadia lay silent. She closed her eyes and Foskett thought she was sleeping. "I'm not dead," she said.

"No, you're not," Foskett answered. "But you would have been."

Nadia opened her eyes and looked at him for the first time. She blinked slowly. "What's going on, Foskett?" she asked.

"You were ... I ..." Foskett thought he would be able to explain. "I ... I got a call from the police that you were in custody. I ... broke you out of jail, sort of. We're at my mother's old house; hopefully where they won't look for us for a while. Though I'm sure they'll figure it out soon enough, so we might not have much time. I think it's our only chance to stop her. Your only chance. My only chance. We ..."

"Stop, please," Nadia said. She lay motionless, breathing deeply.

"Look. I know this is fucked up. It is all fucked up. But it's our only chance. I am going to make you go to sleep, for a long time. I can make you sleep so you can do what you need to do, so you can sort this out and make her go away."

Nadia's eyes snapped open. "You're fucking crazy," she said.

"Listen. I can make you sleep, so you'll have time," he said. Foskett reached into his bag and selected a vial. He read the label, put it back and selected another.

"You have to trust me," she heard.

Nadia lay helpless watching him. She tried to will her arm to move but was trapped inside her body. Another white man telling her to trust him.

"Why?" she felt utterly exhausted.

"Because I have to trust you. You're my only chance. You can go back and stop this ... all of this from taking place. You can stop her. Find help, if you can. Like that man in the park you told me about. Or that one with the long hair—the Viking."

She watched as he prepared a needle. She noticed a bag of liquid suspended from a hook for the first time. The liquid began to drip down a tube he was attaching to her arm.

"You're ..." she started to say. "My mom ..."

"Listen, Nadia," Foskett said. "I'll let your mom know that you're OK. You're going to get us out of this. You're going to go to sleep soon, and then you'll dream and be able to stop her. You have to stop her, Nadia," he said. He could hear how fast he was talking but couldn't stop himself. "This is our only chance. We don't have much time. You have to stop her. I'll be here, watching you. It might take a little while to get these dosages right, but I'll do it. I'll put you asleep so you can dream. I'll stay awake and look after the whole time. Look," he said. Foskett reached back in the bag and withdrew a jar. He took off the lid and shook two pills into his hand. He popped them into his mouth and swallowed.

"See?" he asked. "I couldn't sleep now even if I wanted. I'm looking after you. You need to roll onto your side now," he said. "Oh, sorry. You can't. Here."

Foskett gently pushed Nadia over onto until she faced the wall. She felt something cold and wet at the base of her spine.

"You're going to feel something weird, but it will only last a second. I need you to stay really still," he said.

"What are you doing, Foskett!" Nadia shouted.

"You have to be quiet Nadia!" Foskett hissed. "The neighbor's house is right outside that window! Lie still!"

Nadia felt a piercing pain in her lower back as the needle slipped between vertebrae and entered her spinal column. She felt pressure, and then she felt nothing. Foskett moved the pillow and gently rolled her onto her back. He smoothed her hair and adjusted the sheet around her.

Nadia watched Foskett. His face wavered and blurred. She fought to keep her eyes open but quickly felt herself falling into a blackness without end.

38

*T*he *windows. The windows were wrong. They seemed to point upward into dusty clouds. They let in a dirty light, but little else. A blackboard ran the length of the front wall. Something was written on it. Fuzzy, indecipherable letters. They began to come into focus. A name. The letters spelled a name.*

Nadia sighed in resignation.

"Welcome back, Nadia. Take your time, collect yourself. The class has nothing better to do than wait for you to come to your senses," sarcasm dripped like honey. A familiar voice.

Nadia raised her head and saw Miss Beil glaring at her.

"Pull yourself together, we have a lot to achieve today," she said.

Nadia tasted metal. She probed the top of her mouth with her tongue and pursed her lips. She swallowed but the taste remained. She looked at the desk where she sat. Her hands were resting on the surface. She lifted her right hand and turned it, studying the gold ring on her finger. It meant something. It was important. A tear formed in the corner of her eye. Why couldn't she remember?

Nadia listened to a sound deep in her mind. A distant muttering, somewhere far away. Oh, God, don't die! Don't die! More, she needs a little more. Too much is bad, too much is bad! Words fired like bullets over a far hill. She knew the voice. She had heard it before. But she didn't know where. Nadia touched her eye and looked at the moisture on her finger tip. Was she crying? Her eyes went back to the gold ring. It had three small diamonds embedded in it. She would turn the ring around so people wouldn't know its value. She didn't trust people. Especially ... In God we Trust. What does that mean?

Nadia stared at the woman in front of her. She stood by a large desk in a white dress with black spots. She was frowning. To her right sat a young man in a plaid shirt and dirty denim jeans. Turning her head to the left she saw a blonde girl sitting at a wooden desk, wearing some sort of cheerleader outfit. A bright red 'R' stood on the front of her white sweater. Nadia felt her mind clearing. She licked her lips. It tasted different. She started to remember.

"Shit," she said.

"Indeed, Nadia," Miss Beil said. "I need you totally focused. Are you totally focused now?"

"Yes, ma'am," Nadia lied.

"Today is very important," Miss Beil said. "The convention starts today. And each of you have important work to carry out." Miss Beil opened her desk.

"I have something for each of you. Something special." She reached into the drawer and pulled out a small cloth bag that sat easily in her palm, and pieces of red card. She walked over to where Randall sat and handed him the cards.

"These will get you in. They are tickets to the convention. Don't lose them," she said.

Randall read them, folded them and put them in his back pocket.

"And this is a special present," she said as she placed the small cloth sack on the desk in front of him. He opened it and removed a polished gold lighter. Randall beamed. He turned it slowly in his hand, studying the scene engraved on the surface, a tall sailing ship with its sails unfurled

and bow crashing through waves. He thumbed the flint wheel and gazed into the flame.

"Thank you, Cassie," he said.

Miss Beil gently touched Randall's head. She stroked his hair. "I am so proud of you," she said.

Randall put the lighter back into its pouch. He slid the pouch into his front pocket. He smiled at Miss Beil as he did so.

"Now you run along, and do what you need to do," Miss Beil told him. She stroked his hair one more time before returning to her desk. "Go," she said over her shoulder.

Randall rose from his seat and left the room.

Nadia looked at her hands. She pressed a finger onto the surface of her desk and watched it disappear into the wood. "Fuck fuck fuck fuck fuck fuck, get it right, get it right," she heard in the distance, somewhere deep in her mind. "Don't fuck up, get it right, not too much, don't fuck up, oh, you fuck up," she heard. Foskett, she thought. How can she hear Foskett? She rested her head in her hands, trying to stay in one place, in one reality, trying to stay in the classroom.

"And Nadia, I have something for you too," Miss Beil said.

Nadia lifted her head and watched Miss Beil bring a knife to her desk. "You will need this," she said as she placed the knife in front of Nadia. For a fleeting second Nadia thought of plunging it into Miss Beil's heart.

Miss Beil laughed. "Use that when you need to, and only when you need to," she said. She waited until Nadia pocketed the knife. "Now," she said. "You are my warrior. You have passed your test and shown your loyalty."

"I got things to do now, right?" Nadia asked.

"You do have things to do now, dear," Miss Beil answered. She handed Nadia a ticket to the convention. Nadia placed it in a pocket,

knowing that if she were strong enough, she could simply appear inside the building.

"You need to weasel your way into the Black Caucus and make sure Dawson makes history. Get him to the stage. He'll do it with your help, dear. He'll be the hero, Wallace will be president, and your present will be guaranteed.

"But we all have things to do! Each of you must succeed," she said. "With each piece in place, nothing can stop us! Randall will make sure that fire ends the convention. Off you go, Nadia."

Nadia backed away from the smiling Miss Beil, until she met a wall. She felt the wall start to surround her.

"Now, June," she heard from the room, followed by the familiar smack of ruler against flesh. June muffled her own cry of pain and surprise. "I am worried about you. That's why you make me do this to you. Hannegan must not get his way. Are you able to do what you have to?"

"Yes," June whispered.

Nadia let herself slip all the way through the wall.

*N*adia stumbled onto an empty sidewalk. She walked forward looking for a place to sit. A bus stop. She didn't care where. Her whitened knuckles gripped the metal bench frame. And then she smiled. She felt stronger. She let her hand pass through the steel. She held her hand in front of her, sitting up straighter. She closed her eyes and brought all her attention to her hand.

Fear rose from a deep place within her chest, but she reached an invisible hand down and held the fear at bay. She focused on the fear, as if it were a stone. At first, all she could do was stare at it. She tried to steady her breath, inhaling deeply, exhaling slowly. Inhaling deeply, exhaling slowly. She started to feel around the fear, to explore its edges. She found that the farther away she took her attention, the less she felt, until there was finally none.

She opened her eyes and looked at her hand.

I am in a dream and this is what fear feels like, she thought. The fear is as real as this bench, she realized. I can pass through it. It will soon be in the past. She breathed deeply through her nostrils and sat up straight. Air entered her body, and she exhaled, feeling the warm wind pass over her top lip. She looked at the street in front of her. Green and white buses clattered past. The roar of cars created a wall between herself and the world around her.

"*That's a pretty neat trick," a voice next to her said.*

Nadia flinched. A man in a tweed suit stood before her. She knew the hair under his hat was badly cut. He sat down beside her.

"I am serious. That is a really useful trick," he said. "Did she teach you that?"

"She didn't teach me shit," Nadia answered. "I've always been able to do this."

"That's what I thought," he said. "Can we talk?"

Nadia looked down the street, clear sidewalk either way, busy street in front. She put her hand in the pocket holding the knife, but she didn't feel afraid. Her fear was reserved for Miss Beil. Nadia stared at him.

"Just talk, that's all," the man in tweed said.

"Whatever," Nadia answered.

"You don't look all here. Are you OK?" he asked.

"What are you talking about?" Nadia responded. She looked at her other hand, and turned her palm towards him. "I am here," was all she said. The echoes in the back of her mind were growing distant.

"Yes. I see," he said. "My name is Petrit. I am a dreamer like you. I know you met another dreamer. I have seen him. He is helping you."

"He says never to trust a god," Nadia said.

"Then he understands the real threat. Good," Petrit said. "We may have a chance."

"We?"

"You don't trust Miss Beil. You don't want her to succeed. We have that in common," Petrit said.

Nadia studied his face, weighing his words.

"June isn't very happy," he said.

"You've been talking to her!" Nadia said. "Miss Beil beats her because of you."

"*Miss Beil beats her because Miss Beil is evil,*" Petrit said. "*But June isn't helpless. And neither are you. Miss Beil is a beast. I admit, I don't know what kind of beast, exactly. I know she controls you and others through pain or fear or something. I know that she wants something to happen, that she even needs something to happen. She gains power from how they happen. But she needs you and the others to make that thing happen. She is weak in that way,*" he said.

"*Weak?*" Nadia asked. "*Whatever.*"

"*They need people like you to do their bidding. You can either serve them or you can fight them. There is no middle ground. There are no real victims, and I think you know that. There is always a choice,*" he said.

"*She is going to act soon, isn't she?*" he asked.

Nadia nodded.

"*Then we haven't any time to waste. I am going to walk away now and let you go your own way to do what you will do. I am going to trust that you will do what you feel is the right thing to do. I am choosing to trust you. Once this is all over, I would really like to talk with you more.*"

He stood up and looked down at Nadia.

He gave her his hand, "*What is your name? Do you mind giving it to me?*"

Nadia stared at his hand. She decided to take it.

"*My name is Nadia,*" she said.

"*Nadia,*" he repeated. "*Nadia. Do the right thing.*"

Nadia watched as he walked away, realizing she still knew very little about him. She moved her hand slowly across the bench, watching her fingers melt into the wooden slats beneath her. She shook her head, clearing it. She watched him disappear into the crowded street, only then letting go of the knife pocketed in her dress.

Nadia smiled. She thought of Foskett. It had been a knife that brought them together. She leaned back on the bench and tried to slow her mind, to steady the slow movement to and fro. She felt like she was on a sailing ship, though she had never been off land. She closed her eyes and felt the world spin slowly, focusing on Foskett.

The view was cloudy. She saw a small room filled with a bed and little else. A man checked the arm of a young woman. He was checking her pulse. She could only see the back of his head, his slanting shoulders, his muffin top spilling over his belt. It was Foskett. He was injecting something into the girl's arm. Into her arm. She didn't want to watch.

When she opened her eyes, she saw the busy traffic of the street. A green and white electric bus stopped in front of the bench. Passengers got off; others got on. The bus drove away. She felt her vision growing hazy. She gripped onto the bench and tried to concentrate. Her mind became cloudy. She tried to hold onto awareness. She was dreaming. She needed to be dreaming. A man had spoken to her, a man she didn't trust. Every man she met seemed to insist that she trust him. Nadia slapped her cheek. Concentrate! Focus! There was a plan of sorts. There were different plans. She played a part in each. She ...

Randall. She didn't trust Randall. He was too keen. He said he was afraid of fire but he looked positively rapt with Miss Beil's gift of a lighter. Where was Randall now, Nadia thought. Where was Randall? Go to Randall, she whispered. Nadia closed her eyes and trusted herself.

*R*andall followed the crowd as it moved towards the stadium. At a kiosk he bought a flag. Others were waving theirs, but he had something else in mind.

"Time for some fun!" he said aloud.

A few heads turned to see who had spoken and smiled at him. He grinned back. Weeks of waiting, of watching her train the newbies, of playing his part of confused fellow traveler. Now he got to play. He reached his hand into his pocket and fingered the cloth sack. He wanted to take out the lighter, to feel its polished metal, to study its design, to flick it on and off, on and off. To see that magical little flame dance.

At the stadium entrance on Madison Street he handed over one of his tickets and went inside. He was pushed along with the crowd, shuffling down a corridor. His ticket was for the fifth tier, but once inside he ignored that. So did any security—Randall doubted security even existed in this place. It was going to be easy. But he wanted a view of the ground before he disappeared behind the scene, so he joined the crowded floor. He looked up at the red, white, and blue banners decorating the upper floors. He stared into the faces of presidents past, part of a display that took up one whole end of the stadium. And there at the end was old Franklin D. Folks had come to party. Randall thought it a pathetic excuse to party.

He felt a hand on his shoulder. He turned and was met by a smile.

"Today we'll make it happen, eh! This sign says victory, son! Not just an election, but the whole damn war."

The man thrust a sign at Randall and he took it. Roosevelt and Victory, it said. Randall grinned at the man. Fucking Roosevelt was trying to shaft his vice president, doing it in typical elite fashion—letting others do it for him. If I were at the convention, I would vote for Henry A. Wallace, the president was going to say. Absolute and utter bullshit. He thought of June in her ridiculous sweater with its stupid big 'R' on the front. The old snob would be dead within a year and the right man would succeed him. Still, Randall clutched the sign. Good kindling.

Cassie had let him listen to Wallace, though he couldn't remember everything he had heard. He had opened his eyes in that dream and saw that he was in a room with a fireplace. He sat in a comfortable leather chair. He let his body sink into it. His hands rested on the arms of the chair. He was alone in the room except for a large wooden radio on a table. The voice on it was familiar.

"Some have spoken of the "American Century." It was Wallace at his finest. "I say that the century into which we are entering—the century which will come into being after this war—can be and must be the century of the common man."

The common man, Randall repeated silently.

"When the freedom-loving people march; when the farmers have an opportunity to buy land at reasonable prices and sell the produce of their land through their own organizations; when workers have the opportunity to form unions and bargain through them collectively; and when the children of all the people have an opportunity to attend schools which teach them the truth of the real world when these opportunities are open to everyone, then the world moves straight ahead."

It all sounded so right, Randall thought. He felt an instinctive hatred of privilege, of those who had when too many had nothing. Like himself.

"The search for freedom—The march of freedom of the past 150 years has been a long-drawn-out people's revolution. The people's revolution aims at peace and not at violence, but if the rights of the common man are attacked, it unleashes the ferocity of the she-bear who has lost a cub."

Randall smiled. He knew who the she-bear was, and he liked being her cub. With her he got to fight for that revolution.

"Where are you from, son?" the man asked, snapping Randall back.

"Mississippi!" Randall answered. He liked the sound of that word, and it was the first word that came to mind. Besides, how could anybody respond? With sympathy? He could barely hear himself over the chants and songs each delegation seemed to be playing.

"Look over there—there's your people," the man pointed at a field of signs.

Randall could make out state names, among them Mississippi. He pushed his way through several rows of people until he was lost among them. He looked over his shoulder from a safe distance and couldn't see the man. Then he turned away from his new home state and worked his way out of the melee to an exit. Hours would pass as speech after speech was made. Roosevelt would be nominated, bands would play, but he would need to have everything ready. Location is everything, he thought. Chicago Stadium had lots of places to make a fire, but he had to find where one could cause the most panic and threaten the whole building.

He worked his way off the floor of the stadium and back into the corridor. People streamed past as he studied the walls. He was somewhere near the podium. There had to be an access corridor, an area under the stage or under the seating. He followed the wall until he found what he was looking for. A workman's entrance. He pried open the door and ducked inside. Above him were stairs and bracings. He moved away from the door and worked his way under more seats until he saw what he wanted, a place far enough away from the entrance to be obscured from any workman looking in, but close enough to it to seal it off with flames.

Randall ripped the placard off the stick and broke the stick into fragments. He ripped the card and emptied his pockets—fliers collected as he came in, discarded tickets, crepe paper buntings. He expertly built his pyre. He felt safe and took his time. With a knife he made shavings from one of the braces supporting the seats above him. The marks looked like the gnawing of a rat. He added his other pieces, bit by bit. Over the top he created a teepee of broken sticks, ripped cards and torn flag.

Randall sat back and admired his work. He stared at it, toying with his new lighter. He ran his fingers over the smooth metal. Smelled the sweet flammable fluid within. He flicked the flint wheel and watched the flame play. He blew and the flame went out. Reverently, he put the lighter back into its cloth bag and into his pocket. He didn't have to come back until the next evening, and was looking forward to a bit of fun on the streets before coming back. As soon as he finished what Cassie asked.

41

*N*adia *heard noises, the sounds of many people moving, calling, cheering. She slowly opened her eyes and saw movement. Stepping back, she was engulfed in shadow. The atmosphere around her was contagious, a tangible excitement running through the building. Nadia remained focused. She scanned the people nearby, all of them oblivious to the young woman standing with her back to a wall. She looked in the direction of where they were going, and in the direction from where they had come. From her vantage point a movement caught her eye. A small door under the bleachers above her opened, just enough, allowing somebody to slip out.*

Randall closed the door securely, stood and walked away from the convention floor.

Nadia felt an arm reach across her shoulders and turn her away from Randall. She glanced over and saw a taller man, the profile of a white face.

"So, you took care of that hair," she said.

"It's just under the hat. Every man here wears a hat. Have you noticed that?" Jakob asked.

"Yeah. I did, actually."

"It's a strange custom. They even wear them inside," he said.

Jakob led her to a set of stairs. They climbed them and sat in a gallery that was quickly filling up.

"Are you OK," he asked once they sat. He gently touched her face with the back of his fingers. He was surprised that she let him.

"I'm OK. At least I think I will be. I'm starting to feel better," she said.

"What's going on?" he asked.

"I'm not really sleeping. Well, I am, but it's because of a drug. Foskett—"

"The man you have to see?"

"Yeah, him. He is using something to keep me asleep. Don't look at me like that," she said. "It will work."

"You don't sound so sure," he said. "And you're ... what's the matter with your arm?" he asked.

Nadia lifted her arm awkwardly and examined it as if it were something detached from her body. "I don't know. It feels a bit tingly and numb. It'll be fine," she said opening and closing her hand. "It might be that drip Foskett has me on. He stuck it into my spine."

"You are very brave," he said gently.

"I don't have a choice," Nadia gazed out at the growing crowd. "I ... No. I'm really scared, actually."

"You're not alone, now," he said.

"That's for sure. Our friend showed up again. He's here somewhere. He might even be watching us right now," Nadia said.

"Bad Haircut? I'll find him and try to see what he's up to," Jakob said.

"He said he wants to stop Miss Beil, and that he's been talking with June," Nadia said.

"Do you believe him?" he asked.

"I ... I don't know," she said. "He said his name was Petrit and that he thought Miss Beil was evil."

"I agree with that," Jakob said.

Nadia looked at him. She was glad he was sitting next to her, "I've been practicing my dream yoga."

"That's good," he replied.

"I didn't walk to get here. I closed my eyes and thought it. It felt like I was falling asleep again, but ... different."

"That is impressive," he said. "I was taught that at a monastery, not far from my home. It gave me freedom to ... well, to go deeper. Go where I wanted ..."

"When we can, when there is time, will you take me to learn at one of these monasteries?"

Nadia felt herself relax for the first time in weeks as she watched Jakob smile, "of course I will." He reached over and touched her hand.

"I need to go now and talk to somebody," he said. "I've been avoiding her, but I don't think I have a choice anymore."

"What is she like?" Nadia asked.

"She is beautiful, and strong, and just being around her makes you feel beautiful and strong. Even when you should know better, even when you know you will probably be used like a nameless tool and maybe even die, you still feel that way. I tried to find out who your Miss Beil was on my own, and she pulled me back before it was too late," Jakob was looking at the people taking their seats below them.

"What happened? What did you see?" Nadia asked.

"I don't know," he avoided her gaze. "I really don't. But there was danger. Whatever I saw was pure menace. It was in a terrible place, born of terrible beliefs."

"I tried to find out about her on the computer," Nadia said. "I tried all sorts of names that sounded like hers. One site was about hell and fallen angels."

"Where I went to was a hell realm, that's for sure. I need to learn more. Artemis was there, and she saved me. So I'll ask her. We're going to need her help," Jakob looked at Nadia.

"What are you going to do until tonight? Is there a safe place you can go?" he asked.

"I think there is. I'm going to try to find somebody. I feel like I have to," Nadia fingered the gold ring she wore.

"OK," Jakob said. "Please be safe, and be careful who you trust."

Nadia laughed.

Jakob looked at the seats around them. He took Nadia's hand and led her away, taking her down a corridor until he found a deserted corner. "OK, I am going to close my eyes now. I will see you tomorrow, at the Convention."

"Yes," she said.

Jakob let go of her hand and leaned back against the wall. He winked at her. She watched as he closed his eyes. He seemed to relax. His features softened. His whole body seemed to soften, to lose substance. He grew translucent, until she saw the wall through him. Then he was gone. Nadia lifted her numbed hand to her mouth. She lowered it and smiled.

Nadia walked back to the workman's entrance she saw Randall exit. She leaned into it, letting her body slowly flow through the wood. Once inside she searched under the seating until she found his little pyre. She picked up the kindling with her good arm and scattered it in a far corner. She stuffed the ripped paper and card into her pockets and kicked away the shavings. It might not stop Randall, but would slow him down, and let him know his hide away was discovered.

Once outside she emptied her pockets into a garbage can. Then she leaned against a wall, checked that she was truly alone, and closed her eyes. She fingered the gold ring, nan's ring.

Where are you, nan? Nadia whispered. Where are you? I can't do this without your help.

Randall knew how to ghost through city streets, to be too irrelevant to be noticed. And he knew how to hide from those trying to find him, or those trying to hurt him. Social workers. Safety Officers. Firemen. After Nadia had disappeared, he pushed the newspapers off himself. It was dark, and they were down the corridor. But he was certain of what he had seen, Nadia and a stranger who didn't belong here. Cassie would like to hear about this. He re-entered the workman's entrance before he returned to Cassie and rebuilt his pyre.

42

June left the classroom holding her face and sobbing. She stopped at the first glass fronted shop and looked at her reflection. She gently ran her fingers down her smooth cheeks. Miss Beil couldn't know what was deep within her heart, surely she couldn't. That's why she used fear, that's the only reason why somebody would use fear, to control what they can't know. June wiped the tears from her face and walked down the sidewalk, looking back at the door to the building housing the classroom until she turned a corner and couldn't see it anymore.

Miss Beil enjoyed toying with her, hurting her, manipulating her. That was more terrifying. Because it was crazy. Nothing she could do could please crazy.

June hailed a taxi and went straight to the Stevens Hotel. She asked for Johnnie's room number at reception, took the elevator to Johnnie's floor, found his door, and knocked.

Johnnie opened the door. He looked at June and smiled. June rushed into his arms before she started to cry.

"What is it, my dear?" Johnnie asked.

"I'm just so happy to see you," June said.

"Well, you can cry for being happy. I don't ever want you to cry because you're sad. I want my June to be happy always."

He said 'my June', June thought. She sniffed and wiped her eyes on Johnnie's shoulder. He pushed her away at arm's length.

"A cheerleader for Roosevelt!" he said. "What a beautiful get up!"

"I'm your cheerleader, Johnnie," June said. She sounded corny, but didn't care. Johnnie liked it, that was all that mattered. He drew her close again and held her tight.

"I missed you so much," he said.

"I missed you too," June said.

Johnnie guided June into the room and closed the door. He drew her close again and they kissed. She started undoing his shirt buttons while he pulled her sweater over her head. They didn't say another word until afterwards, spooning under thin hotel sheets.

"I love you," he whispered into her ear.

"I love you," June said, staring across the room.

"I'm in the middle of the making of history, June. You wouldn't believe it. I'm in the eye of the storm, watching it all happen, a ring side seat, even playing a role in making the next president. And what makes it all matter is knowing you are in my life," he said.

June smiled even though Johnnie couldn't see.

"I think we make a great pair, is what I'm saying. I think with you by my side I can do anything. What I'm saying is ... I want you by my side, June."

June felt Johnnie's breath on her shoulder. She fought back tears. She felt loved and wanted and safe and wanted to savor every moment of it. "Tell me about your week," she said.

"It was wild. Absolutely unbelievable. Bob's in the thick of it, so I'm right there with him. We had a meeting at a hotel and all the party bosses were there. And they chose the next President, just like that. Bob has it all planned," Johnnie said.

"I thought Roosevelt was the president?" June asked.

"He is, cupcake, but, well, he isn't very well. I don't think anybody expects him to make it through the full term. So whoever is vice president will have to step up. That's what it's all about. It's not choosing a vice president when the president is going to die. Whoever is chosen will be t he next president. After Roosevelt."

"Tell me about it," June said.

"They were all in the hotel room—my boss Bob, Edwin Pauley—he's the oilman, a very powerful person, real mover and shaker. He was in an airplane crash and was told he'd spend the rest of his life in a wheelchair, but not Pauley, nothin' can keep him down. He's real close to FDR, I mean real close. There was Pa, that's what he's called, but his real name is Edwin Watson. Major General Edwin Watson. Real intimidating guy. He's the type of guy who makes kings, and I got to meet him," Johnnie s aid.

"You're going to make a wonderful king," June said.

Johnnie breathed in the scent of June's hair before talking again. "Even the mayor was there, old Kelly himself. That type of politician has had his day. I can tell you that here, and everybody knows it out there, but nobody will say it out loud."

"Be careful, love," June said.

Johnnie kissed the back of her head, "I am. There's thinking something, and there's saying something. I'm learning from the masters."

"Who else was there?" she asked.

"A guy named Allen. George, I think. He came from the same swamp as Kelly. When I grow up I'm gonna drain that swamp," he said.

"You are grown up," she whispered, wriggling into his warm body.

"You make it hard to focus," he said.

"Tell me, what happened," June said, adjusting pillows around her.

"Ok, Ok, you asked for it. Comfy?" he asked.

"With you, always," June said.

"So," Johnnie said, "we met in this fancy hotel room somewhere upstairs."

"*It was the type of room that has its own name. I've never seen anything like it and don't even want to think about what it would cost to stay there for a night. But these guys don't need to care about money. All the big wigs in the Party were there, the real power behind the throne. I stood behind Bob. Pauley sat across from him. Pa sat with his back to the fireplace—the room had its own fireplace! Kelly had a chair but seemed to pace around more than sit. He looked soft, but his mouth was like a shotgun loaded with rusty nails. All Allen did was sit and smoke his fat cigar, taking everything in. But when he spoke, everybody had to listen.*"

"*The President's tired,*" Bob started. The leather chair creaked as he leaned forward. "*He's ailing. He's ill. He's not going to bounce back. He never recovered from that trip to Tehran,*" he said.

"*His weight is dropping. Who knows, it could be cancer,*" Pauley added.

"*McIntire's been mis-diagnosing him. Bruenn says it's his heart,*" Pa added.

"*Let's just agree that the President's doctors shouldn't be trusted. What we all know is that he'll win a fourth term, he just isn't going to survive it,*" Bob said.

"We all thought it, we all knew it," Johnnie told June. "But nobody likes to say it."

"It's impossible to talk to him," Bob said. "His ego blocks the way and he enjoys keeping you guessing. We're going to have to do this without him. You can't tell what he'll do."

"So we'll do it," Pauley said. "We have the man. He's reliable. He's—"

"He's a dunce," Kelly growled.

"Now that's not fair!" Pauley said.

"Well," Kelly said, "He's not Wallace, and that's all that matters, isn't it?"

Kelly was staring at Bob, trying to intimidate him or act like some alpha dog, just because we were in his city. He runs this place like his own fiefdom, Johnny explained to June. He even bans books he doesn't like. I watched Bob handle it. His face turned red and I watched him work his jaw muscles. But he kept his mouth closed, let others fight it out and come to his way of thinking.

That's when I jumped in, Johnnie told June. "The President's already chosen Truman," I said.

"The President did what he was told, for once," Allen said. "He wasn't even in his right mind when Edwin and Pa cornered him."

"Truman is the designated heir," Allen continued. "You got your man, Hannegan. I don't understand why you're so testy about it."

I watched Bob's jaw muscle work. He got his man, and his way, but he just can't stand Allen. Allen is sharp like a knife, a useful tool but also a weapon. He's the type of Washington insider that doesn't go away. Bob looked at Pauley and Pa and relaxed a little. He got what he wanted, and he used his allies well. In the Oval office that day Pauley and Pa achieved what Bob thought was impossible. Byrnes, the so called 'Assistant President' was champing at the bit and only Pauley could keep him in check. And to handle FDR to boot—I would have loved to have been a fly on the wall for that meeting.

"For better or for worse," Pa said, "we have our man. So set your personality differences aside and focus on the business at hand. Byrnes will still try for the nomination. He won't stand for a fake southerner from a border state like Truman to steal it. And Wallace—"

"And Wallace will win any honest vote," Kelly interrupted. "Don't look at me like that gentlemen, I am only stating the obvious." He was looking straight at Bob. "Hannegan here made sure Harry got nominated for his senate seat in '40, he'd no doubt do the same again for a bigger prize."

All eyes went to Bob. He's a shrewd player, my boss! As senator, it was Truman who positioned him as party chairman, and coached him in how to let the President think it was his own idea.

"It's true, Wallace will win any honest vote," he said, staring back at Kelly. "But only once." He let the words sit between them before continuing. "We all know Wallace will carry the convention if we don't guide it properly. Hell, he's by far the most popular candidate. And all eyes will be on us. I say let Wallace win the first vote, let him take the first day. He'll relax, he'll go back to his hotel smiling. And the next day he won't know what hit him."

Bob sat back, waiting for them to ask for more. It didn't take long.

"And what will hit him, Bob? Henry wants it bad and he won't just lie down," Kelly asked.

"No, he won't," Bob responded. "He'll plot how to outflank Byrnes. Maybe he'll notice the door that's closed to him, the one we'll be behind, but by that time it'll be too late. As long as Wallace isn't nominated at the end of the day, then he's finished."

"You're going to let Wallace win the vote in the first round?" Kelly asked.

"Of course, he'll win the first vote—he's the most popular choice. There is no way he can lose it, which is why we'll let the first vote take place."

"Give the baby his ball is what you're saying," Kelly said.

"Yes. Exactly. The people at the convention, including Wallace, need to believe that their every vote counts. On the second day we'll count those votes until we win. It's already been decided. Wallace is out and Truman is in. After the first vote, but before Wallace can be formally nominated, we shut down proceedings using any excuse. We identify who will try to rush the nomination—we know who we're talking about. And we stop them. My outstanding assistant here knows how to do that. You were boxer at Notre Dame, were you not, Johnnie?" he asked me.

I did box, June, I never told you that. But they all looked at me. "Yes sir," I said. "Senator Pepper will be detained."

"Easy now!" Pauley said.

"He's only joshing, Edwin," Bob said. "Johnnie is now a practicing lawyer. He'll simply talk to Claude and distract him." They all laughed at that—at me. But I just smiled at them.

"And," Bob went on, "Jackson has strict instructions." Senator Jackson is the chair of the convention, hun. "There will be no nomination until we're ready. Even if he has to adjourn the whole damn show."

They all looked at him, taking in what he said. Just adjourn the whole damn show, that's what he said, and June, that's the kind of gumption he has.

"I'm not saying it will be easy," Bob added. "We'll all be working through the night promising sweets and lollies, ambassadorships, postmaster positions, cash ... anything it takes."

"That's the answer Bob!" Pa held his belly as he laughed. "Just throw candy at 'em from the back of the truck and they'll do whatever you want."

The others in the room smiled out of politeness, knowing it was the truth. And that was the meeting, the plan of action. I'll probably be busy all night tomorrow. Well, I will be, I mean. Very busy.

June turned around and nestled into his chest.

"Johnnie?" she asked.

"Yes, my love?"

"I need to ask you to do something for me tonight," June said. "I can't explain why, but I need you to do it."

"Anything," he said as he stroked her hair.

44

Nadia opened her eyes and saw a sturdy wooden door. She swayed slightly on her feet. Her legs were reluctant, but they finally stepped forward. She climbed the short stairway to the door. All she had to do was knock, and the door would open. She looked at the ring on her finger. Her hand lay at an odd angle against her thigh. She tried to raise it but couldn't. She closed her eyes for the briefest moment and the world began to spin. The wood in front of her eyes blurred and she realized she was falling through it. Nadia collapsed on the floor of a tidy living room.

"Oh my!" she heard. Nadia felt arms around her and the sensation of being lifted to a sitting position. "Oh my!" she heard again. "You are a heavy girl!"

Her nan walked away and returned with a glass full of water. Nadia reached for it, forgetting her arm was useless and the water splashed onto her face. She shook her head, coughing, and the woman went to the kitchen and returned with another glass. She threw the water into Nadia's face before kneeling in front of her. The woman cocked her head in thought, and raised her hand. Nadia felt a sharp slap across her cheek and the room tilted to the side.

"What are you doing!" Nadia cried.

"That's better," her nan said smiling. "I lose you sometimes," she said. "You just shimmer and disappear." The woman dabbed at Nadia's face with her night dress. She pulled Nadia to a more upright position.

"You just stay with me now. Then you can explain what this is all about." The woman smiled and pulled a chair over to sit directly in front of Nadia. "I have dreamt of you," she told Nadia. "One of us is dreaming now," she said. She leaned close to Nadia. "I'm not quite sure which, to be honest."

Her nan sat back and giggled.

"I am," Nadia said.

"I know, dear. I just wanted to make sure you knew," she smiled. "Why do you never come? I wait for you beside the tree, but you—"

"That was my mom. She told me her dream. She knew you were waiting, but she was too scared to go to you. You were waiting by a big tree, she said, and—"

"So that was her," her nan said. "Your mother. She felt like a part of me, a lost part. So that would make you a part of me as well."

"Your ring," Nadia said. "Show me your ring, please."

The woman lifted her left hand for Nadia to see. On her ring finger was a gold band with three small diamonds. Her nan looked at Nadia's finger. She took Nadia's hand and examined the gold ring.

"Well. Isn't that something," the woman said.

"You are Ruby," Nadia said. "You tell your grandchildren about your dreams, and they will tell their children. But their dreams sometimes scare them." Nadia felt tears run down her cheeks.

"But not you. You believe in dreams and you were brave enough to come," she studied Nadia. "What is the matter with you, child? Why can't you move?"

"I don't know. It might be because of what is keeping me here. But ... I don't know. Nothing feels right anymore. It feels like I am running out

of time, and I can't do anything about it. Like it's too late," Nadia cried freely.

"It's never too late, child, and you know that. Now stop that crying. You came here because you knew I could help you," Ruby raised her hand and slapped Nadia again. "You have to stay with me, girl!"

"Nadia," Nadia said. "My name is Nadia."

"Nadia. That is a beautiful name. Who gave you that name?" Ruby asked.

"My mom. Amy. Your granddaughter," Nadia said.

"Well," Ruby said, holding Nadia's eyes to keep her attentive. "I can't wait to meet her. When my daughter has a daughter!" Her expression changed and she wore a serious look on her face. "But you've come to me in a dream. I'm pretty sure it's your dream. I can get real confused at times, but I'm not now. There's something we have to do today. That's why you're here. The night's already gone, and you need my help obviously, you can hardly move."

"Tell me," Ruby said. "What do you need me to do?"

"You have to go to the convention," Nadia said. "There's a ticket in my pocket. Take it."

Ruby reached into Nadia's back pocket and removed the red pass.

"You have to find Dawson. Congressman Dawson. Don't let him reach the stage. That's really important. He's going to try to help Wallace win the nomination—"

"Isn't that a good thing, child?"

"No. I mean I don't know. He wins where I am from, and I don't ever want to go back to that place. And she wants him to win, so we have stop him. Just don't let Dawson get to the stage. She wants him to get to the stage, and she … she's not right. She's evil. And Randall's going to start a fire. A lot of people will die. They do die. Tell them it's under the

bandstand, beneath the stage." Nadia stopped talking and gasped for breath. Even moving her chest was difficult.

Ruby wiped Nadia's face and stroked her hair. "You just settle down. You came to me. You're my family, and you're asking for my help. I don't understand a lot of what of what you said, but I'll do it, Nadia, don't worry. I'll go to your convention. Just try to stay with me, dear," she said.

Nadia looked at her great grandmother, at the smooth brown skin of her cheeks, and the shiny brown hair framing her face. "Tell me about the tree," Nadia whispered.

"The tree is everything. It is the entire universe. Its roots reaching to the essence of life, binding all life together. Its branches reach into infinite potential. Every branch a world in itself, continually growing and branching even more. The trunk connects them all, holding all life together."

"Can you prune the tree? Can you cut off a branch?" Nadia asked.

"Is that what you really want to do, Nadia?"

"Yes," Nadia admitted. "I want to prune that tree." Tears filled Nadia's eyes and spilled down her cheeks.

"OK, child, then that is what we will do." Ruby stroked Nadia's cheek. "We'll prune the tree. We'll make it grow in a different direction. You are starting to fade, Nadia. Stay with me."

"I need to see Jakob," Nadia said. Jakob, she thought. Jakob.

Ruby watched as Nadia grew translucent and slowly disappeared. "Oh my," was all she said. She looked at her hands, examining each knuckle. She turned them over and followed the lines in her palm. Finally, she decided that she was indeed awake. She changed into her nicest dress, grabbed her coat and handbag, and left the house.

45

*J*akob folded his hands on his chest and breathed deeply. He calmed his mind and surrounded himself in blackness. He felt all thought fade, save one, an intention. Her.

He opened his eyes and squinted in the glare of the midday sun. He followed a familiar stone path past covered stalls. Vendors sold everything from dried meats to religious trinkets. He stopped and looked at one stall, rows of porcelain figures, a woman with arms outspread and multiple breasts. He smiled and shook his head.

He walked to the end of the lane, ignoring those around him. Rounding the corner, he began the short climb up the stairs. At the top was a temple. A magnificent temple, built for her, and where she would be waiting, because he had asked her to wait there. Jakob climbed the last stair and saw the great columns of marble rising to the sky, over a hundred marble columns stretching nearly fifty feet in the air. Each one stood on a huge stone base, painted blue, supporting the great roof, providing a forest of stone columns for the penitents to wander through amazed. He smelled the smoke of incense, and a faint odor of blood. Sacrifices to her. There always had to be blood.

He walked as if drawn by an invisible force, across the courtyard surrounding the temple to a small lane leading away. Among the pilgrims making their way to where he had just left, he saw the unmistakable *glow of her presence. He always wondered why those around could not also see it. Did they simply see a woman sitting at a table, drinking wine from a goblet? How could they not feel her? There she sat. Her blond hair flowed past her bare shoulders. She wore a thin white gown, clasped at the shoulder with a golden broach. Her tanned skin emanated health and vitality.*

Jakob sat in the seat opposite. On the table in front of him stood a goblet full of red wine.

"Drink," she said smiling. And he did.

Jakob finished and sat the goblet down. Despite his best intentions, he was smiling.

"Jakob," she said. "You come to me. I am honored."

Jakob gazed into her eyes and could feel himself slipping, as if on a precipice, the ledge of an endless chasm, urging him to let go and simply fall. He looked down at his hands.

"I come because I need your help," he said. He couldn't explain, or understand why, but he felt like crying.

"And you shall have it, Jakob," she said.

He lifted his eyes and saw her smiling. "Jakob, I do not hide what I am and what I want. Drink," she instructed, and the goblet in front of Jakob was full once again.

He picked it up and smelled the rich scent of fermented grape. He took a sip and felt it slowly flow over his tongue and down his throat. He thought once again of blood and set the goblet down.

"Live fully, that is all I ask of my followers. Savor every moment, every ecstasy, every orgasmic breath. Every morning, every feast, every kill. You know this Jakob, that is why you are here with me, that is why you are bound to me. I will help you, Jakob. This beast you have found does not love life. It festers and feeds on hate and fear. It feeds on death. So that is what we will give it."

All sounds ceased as she spoke. When she had finished Jakob slowly became aware of movement around him, the murmurs of pilgrims, the chirps of birds, the sound of feet on stone. He lifted his goblet and drank deeply, enjoying the taste of the wine, the warmth as the liquid filled him.

"Thank you," he said.

"My dear Jakob. Will you stay and worship?" she asked.

She was teasing.

"No," he said. "I must go and help a friend."

46

*P*etrit sat on a bench near a green space, taking advantage of the shade offered by a nearby ash tree. He liked these little green pockets that cities set aside and protected, little areas of calm in the hustle and bustle of daily life. He took off his fedora and ran his fingers through his unevenly cut hair. He entertained, for the briefest of moments, the thought of visiting one of those places with the large chairs and the red and white and blue striped pole rotating around outside. It was irrational, he thought, feeling guilt or shame at letting another cut one's hair. But culture and custom run deep. As enjoyable, or as releasing, as the experience might be, he knew he would leave feeling somehow soiled.

He watched the young woman in the white sweater walk along the street. Her sleeves were pushed up to her elbows, a long plain skirt covered her legs. Her hair was tied at the back. Such strange cultures and customs.

She sat next to him, meeting his gaze with tired but happy eyes.

"Petrit," she said. "I did as you said. I had Johnnie wake me every time I started to doze. I asked him to stay up all night with me. And he did. He didn't ask why. I kept it in my mind, focused on it all night, the one thought, the thought of staying. But like you said, I stayed here. I stayed awake. Is that all it will take? Am I going to be able to stay here?"

"This is now your home," he said.

"Johnnie is so tired today. He had to go in to work. It's a huge day for him!"

Petrit held her hand. "He sounds like a good man."

"Oh, he is. He is such a good man," June said. "I know I've known him for only a short time, but I know. I just know."

"You are in love," Petrit said.

"I am," June said.

"What will happen to me?" she asked after a pause. "I mean, my body, back there?"

"I imagine your people will look after you. They'll wonder why you never wake up, why you are in some sort of a coma. But sometimes people just don't wake up. From what you have told me, they'll look after you or put your sleeping body in an institution or some kind of hospital, hooked up to different types of monitors, until your body expires, or…"

"She can't hurt me now, can she?" June asked.

"She can't hurt you if you don't fall into her grasp. You are not falling anymore," Petrit said.

"And this is now my life?"

"You know the answer to that, June," Petrit squeezed June's hand and let it go.

"I can't tell you how happy you've made me. I can't thank you enough. I'll never be able to repay you," she said.

"June, you deserve what you have. You made it happen. Your strength made it happen."

June smiled. She sat and watched the wind play through the leaves of the tree above. She listened to the sounds of the city.

"June," Petrit interrupted. "You still have to be strong. There is a lot to do today. She is still here. You have to keep Johnnie alert. Stay with him. Make sure he does what he needs to do. It will be your turn to keep him

awake. *Your futures depend on it. I cannot stress that enough,"* he said. *"Do you know why I trust you, June?"*

June looked at Petrit but didn't respond.

"It is because you ... Let me try to explain. Many people live their lives and never get tested. They never have to fight for their lives, or never have to run for their lives. So, they never learn what type of person they really are. To have their character really tested. Many choose the easiest path or they choose the wrong side. They fail their test of character. You didn't fail June. No matter what she did to you, or what she made you do ..."

He smiled, "You are a good person, June. You are a strong and loving person. You deserve to be happy." Petrit looked out at the city. "And you will be. When we succeed. We still have important work to do to stop the events that created your reality. Miss Beil gets strength from blind faith. Those who fear a god also fear a devil, and that is who I think Cassey Beil serves. This is where we push back and make things turn out differently."

As if on cue, they both stood.

"Miss Beil is going to be so mad," June said.

"She is going to be a little more than that," Petrit let out a laugh.

"Now find Johnnie. Stay by his side, like you will be for years to come."

June smiled and felt a flood of warmth flow through her. "What are you going to do?" she asked.

"I am going to find somebody, another dreamer. He has made contact with Nadia. I hope we can work together. We would be stronger that way," Petrit knit his brows. "Come, it's time we get to work."

Petrit took June in his arms and held her close for a brief moment. Pushing her away he said, "Go. I have been honored to know you, June Clavern."

June Vaughn, she thought. She turned in the direction of the stadium, fingering the special pass Johnnie had given her.

Petrit waited until she had walked away before he, too, went towards the convention. He would find Jakob there.

47

Nadia tried to open her eyes, but they wouldn't respond. They were no longer hers. She felt herself dissolving into a million separate pieces, none belonging to her. She felt fear. Miss Beil was wrong about Nadia's nightmare, when she cast Nadia to frozen wastes, and sun scorched deserts, and finally tormented her with pain in attempts to break her student. Nadia was terrified of the empty solitude before her, of nothingness. The pain of the ants helped distract her. Now she felt real fear, teetering on the precipice of nothingness.

"No no no no no no no!" she screamed without sound. She searched about for purchase, something to hold onto. She saw a hazy light, dimming in the distance. She focused all her attention on the light. It began to grow in intensity and clarity until she could discern shapes within it. The light continued to grow until it surrounded her.

She saw a bed in a small room. A young woman lay motionless on it. A clear tube ran from her arm to a bag suspended beside her. A disheveled man stood over her. He hit his head with his hand again and again. He was shouting at the girl, though Nadia could hear no sound. He walked away from the girl, a few short paces to the opposite wall. He walked back to the girl and shook her, shouting. He tilted her head back and opened her mouth. Leaning down he covered her mouth with his. Her chest rose as he filled it with his own breath. Stepping back, he made a fist and brought it down hard in the center of the girl's chest.

Nadia felt the shock in her own chest. Everything felt more real.

"You son of a bitch, Foskett. Do not kill me!" she thought, clarity returning.

Foskett reached into a small bag, pulled out a syringe and a small vile of yellow liquid. He prepared the syringe and plunged it into the girl's neck. Her eyes opened and she gasped. Nadia looked into her blank eyes, knowing the girl was elsewhere, in another time and place looking down at the scene. Looking at herself. Foskett reached into the bag again and filled the syringe with another liquid. He stabbed the needle into her neck again and the girl closed her eyes. He took her pulse and counted.

Sweat dripped from Foskett's brow. His shirt was drenched under his arms and around his neck. He paced to the wall again and back to Nadia on the bed. To the wall and back to the bed. To the wall and back to the bed. His swiped the surface of the nearby chest of drawers, sweeping anything on it to the floor. He took a smaller pouch out of his medicine bag and emptied it on the surface. He scooped powder out of the bag with a spoon, bit the tip of a tube of sterile water and poured it into the spoon. Using his lighter he heated the spoon, stirring the powder with his syringe to help it dissolve.

Foskett drew the solution up into the syringe. He smiled as he tapped the side and gently pressed the plunger until a small drop appeared at the tip of the needle. He pulled a rubber tube out of his bag and wrapped it tightly around his arm. After clenching and unclenching his fist, he slapped his forearm. He released the tube and inserted the needle into a raised vein, slowly emptying the syringe.

Foskett stumbled to the wall, the needle protruding from his arm and a look of bliss on his face. He slid to the floor. His eyes closed and his body began to convulse. His mouth opened and he gasped once, then stopped breathing.

Foskett dying didn't make any sense. She had seen him in the future. He had died there! Nadia closed her eyes, wanting to flee the scene. She heard the sound of people and went towards the noise.

48

"*Now we have come to the most extraordinary election in the history of our country. Three times the Democratic Party has been led to victory by the greatest liberal in the history of the United States. The name Roosevelt is revered in the remotest corners of this earth. The name Roosevelt is cursed only by Germans and Japs and certain American troglodytes.*"

Wallace smiled broadly as he waited for the crowd to stop cheering. As the wave of sound passed, he leaned into the bank of microphones and continued.

"*By nominating Franklin Roosevelt, the Democratic Party is again declaring its faith in liberalism,*" *he said.* "*Roosevelt is a greater liberal today than he has ever been. His soul is pure. The high quality of Roosevelt liberalism will become more apparent as the war emergency passes. The only question ever in Roosevelt's mind is how best to serve the cause of liberalism in the long run. He thinks big. He sees far.*"

Wallace paused again as the crowd erupted in cheers. This part of the evening was going according to plan.

"*The future must bring equal wages for equal work regardless of sex or race!*" *the speaker had to pause once again as his words were drowned out by the shouts of the crowd.*

"As head of the Iowa delegation, in the cause of liberalism, and with a prayer for prompt victory in this war, permanent peace, and full employment, I give you Franklin D. Roosevelt."

The crowd roared its approval, standing to give the speaker an ovation. Delegates leaped from their seats. It was the most gripping speech they had heard yet. Party leaders were pleased, the first order of business complete. They called the President in San Diego and told him the news. He phoned and spoke to the convention from the west coast.

"What is the job before us in 1944? First, to win the war—to win the war fast, to win it overpoweringly. Second, to form worldwide international organizations, to make another war impossible within the foreseeable future. And third, to build an economy for our returning veterans and for all Americans—which will provide employment and decent standards of living."

There was a resounding cheer. As it settled down another cheer erupted. Voices from the galleries and the floor started demanding the next order of business, nominating the vice president.

"We want Wallace! We want Wallace!" they heard. This time the sound was deafening. Wallace's supporters were there in the thousands, waving placards reading 'Keep the winning team! Roosevelt and Wallace' and 'The people want Wallace'. The speaker was hijacked and Wallace's campaign song began to play. "Iowa, Iowa, that's where the tall corn grows!"

The first ballot was taken and Wallace won easily, but not by the necessary majority. A second vote was needed to secure his place in history.

Ruby felt herself being jostled in the crowd. She grabbed a shoulder to stay on her feet. Dawson was in sight. He was fighting his way through the crowd towards her, or so she thought. She was between Dawson and the stage. As he neared, she felt herself slip. Before she fell arms grabbed her.

"We have to get to the stage!" Dawson shouted to his staffer over the noise of the crowd. Dawson had an eye for history, and as soon as he saw what was developing made a beeline for the podium. The second ballot had to be called. His staffer blazed a path through the crowd. They were calling for Wallace, and if he could make it to the stage and nominate Henry A. for the vice-presidential ticket, they would not only carve a place in history, but in the party as well.

But Ruby had reached Dawson and grabbed his arm. He stared at Ruby, her desperate eyes holding him in place. Dawson shook off his staffer's hand and looked down at her.

"Congressman Dawson, we're all in danger!" shouted Ruby. "There's going to be a fire!"

"There's a guy going to start a fire!" she shouted at the Congressman.

Dawson continued to stare at her. "Look around!" she shouted over the noise. "He's going to burn down the convention!"

The words hit Dawson like a slap and he leaned in close. "What are you saying?" he asked.

"A fire—he's going to start a fire and kill everybody—thousands! You have to stop him!" Ruby called.

"Who? Where is this person?" Dawson asked.

"Under the bleachers, there's a small door. He's got it all set up. You have to stop him!" Ruby's throat hurt from shouting.

Dawson turned to his staffer. "Did you hear that? Go and find that door! I'll warn Jackson!"

Dawson grabbed his staffer, who was torn between the podium and his boss's new order. Dawson shouted at him, "do as I say!"

Dawson forced his feet to move and fought his way through the crowd. The convention chairman had to know they were all in danger.

***

Senator Claude Pepper of Florida had an eye on history, and he knew history was being made. The crowd was hungry, and he was adept at reading crowds. The crowd wanted Wallace, and he was going to give them Wallace. Without a moment's hesitation he started fighting his way to the podium.

Two people blocked his way. The first he recognized. Hannegan's man. They all had a man, an acolyte doing their every bidding. The other was a young blonde woman wearing some sort of cheerleader's outfit. She wore a white sweater with a big 'R' on it.

"Senator Pepper! Senator Pepper! We need to talk with you!" Hannegan's lackey said.

"Out of my way, man!" Pepper shouted.

"Please, sir, this is important!" the young man said, grabbing onto Pepper's sleeve.

"Remove your hands!" Pepper said. He grabbed Johnnie's hand and pried it away. He stepped forward only to find the young woman in his way.

"Please, sir!" she pleaded.

Pepper paused. He met her eyes. There was something amiss. There was something about her that wasn't ...

"Senator Pepper, you have to listen to Johnnie!" she said.

At the mention of the name the spell was broken. Pepper pushed past both of them and struggled to the podium. But the delay was sufficient. He was mere steps away when he heard the gavel sound as Jackson called the convention to a close citing a fire risk.

49

R andall was hunting. He knew his prey was close, and he knew it was vulnerable. Miss Beil had said to knife the long-haired hipster, and that was just what he was going to do. Knife the long-haired hipster, then knife the guy with the bad haircut, and then start the fire.

The first wasn't hard to find. Randall knew he would want to re-enter the convention, so he waited near Madison. It was a side street, perfect for what he needed to do. And just as he expected, his target was walking right towards him.

"Hey! You! Yeah, you!" Randall shouted. Randall walked towards Jakob. As he approached, he reached into his pocket. Before Jakob could react, Randall pulled out a knife and plunged it into Jakob's stomach. Too easy, Randall thought.

Jakob felt a piercing pain as the blade entered and instinctively clutched the wound. Randall smiled at him, but then his face contorted in confusion and pain. Randall dropped his knife and fell to his knees. Behind him stood a man in a tweed suit holding a bloody knife. Randall looked up at Jakob.

"Fuck," he said. "I really liked it here."

Randall fell onto the sidewalk. Jakob watched Randall's body grow translucent and disappear as he died in this reality. Jakob fell to his own knees and looked at his blood-soaked hands. Petrit stood above him.

"Don't you dare leave," he said. "We need to talk."

Jakob became weak. He leaned against the building. He could feel his life ebbing away.

"Make a fist and stick it into the wound," Petrit said. "That will buy you some time. Don't you dare leave," he said again. "I will be back as soon as I can. This isn't finished yet."

Jakob forced his fist into the hole made by Randall's knife. He winced with the pain.

"We?" he asked.

"Just hold on," Petrit said before walking away towards the entrance of the stadium. "Wait for me."

Wait, Jakob thought, and winced as he laughed.

***

Miss Beil looked up to see somebody else in the classroom.

"Artemis," she said. "What brings you to these lowly depths?"

"Kazbiel. The one who lies to God. Up to your tricks again, I see, torturing children to get your way. It was the stench of sulfur and feces that brought me hither. How can you stand your own smell?"

"Smell?" Miss Beil asked. "All that fills my nostrils is the reek of rancid menstrual blood that seems to follow you everywhere."

"You know nothing of fertility or life. You wallow in a cesspit of death and despair," Artemis said.

The two stood for a moment staring distastefully at each other.

"Shall we begin?" the fallen angel said. Her dress fell away as she grew in height, revealing tarnished and dented armor. Dirty wings rose from her back. She let them stretch to their full length and flexed them. Her

eyes grew red. Power surged down her arm and she gripped a long sword tightly.

Artemis took a step and steadied herself. She reached back and took an arrow out of the quiver slung over her shoulder. She lifted the bow that materialized in her hand and placed the arrow on the string. She pulled back, smiling at her enemy.

***

Nadia thought of Jakob, and she found herself beside him, slumped against the stone wall of the stadium. He was pale and his hands were covered in his own blood. Nadia sat beside him, her limbs useless and her face palsied. He tried to smile, but it hurt too much. She tried to smile, but her mouth wouldn't cooperate.

"You look terrible," he said.

"Thanks," she said. Nadia watched her leg slowly sink into the pavement. "Not so hard after all."

"You're a natural," Jakob said.

"Will you take me to those monasteries you talked about? Like you promised?" she asked.

"They'll be expecting you," Jakob said. "What's happening to you?"

"I don't know," she said.

"She's in between realities," they heard above them. "That could be a good thing. But who knows what she'll wake up to. Something must have changed tonight. All I saw at the convention center were hundreds of people leaving," he sat down next to the two. "June played her part perfectly. Senator Pepper never reached the stage."

"Pruning. Fucking. Trees," Nadia whispered.

"Who are you?" Jakob asked.

"My name is Petrit. You may not believe me, but we are on the same side. Well, I would like you to be with us. Both of you. If the gods are going to manipulate us, we can at least fight back. And we're stronger together."

"Nice trick," he said to Nadia.

"She's a natural," Jakob said. "Walks through walls. Goes where she wants. She's a dream yogi. She just needs to learn how to control it better …" He coughed and blood trickled out the corner of his mouth.

"You don't have very much time, my friend. We will have to meet another time. Look," he said pointing. "They've started."

Nadia and Jakob gazed at the horizon. Tall thunder heads covered the distant sky. Angry flashes of lightning illuminated the clouds, made more ominous by the total silence that followed.

"It's called dry thunder. But we know the cause. This is the best way for us. Let the gods fight themselves rather than play with us. Just sit back and watch the mayhem. Such a wonderful show."

"I asked for some help," Jakob said.

"Well done." Petrit smiled at Jakob.

Jakob tried to smile back. His face relaxed and his eyes went blank. Nadia and Petrit watched as an empty space formed between them.

"I think you are soon to follow, Nadia. Whatever is keeping you here is weakening," Petrit said. "Look," he pointed at the clouds. "Absolutely beautiful! Stunning! Look at them go at it!"

Nadia watched the distant lights play across the horizon. "That's Miss Biel up there?" she asked.

"That's whatever Miss Beil was," he said. "Things didn't work out her way this time. The reality she was trying to protect isn't going to occur."

"What's going to happen now?" Nadia asked.

"*That I don't know,*" Petrit answered. "*When you wake up things might be a little different. Hopefully for the better.*"

Nadia looked at Petrit and smiled. Then she watched the sky until her world went dark.

“**N**adia, wake up!”

Nadia slowly opened her eyes. She saw a familiar room: her yellow comforter, pictures on the wall, artwork found and copied from magazines. Her stereo. Books. The picture of her father standing in its frame.

She rubbed her eyes and looked at her wall again, a poster of a beautiful black face, surrounded by a halo of hair. Strong cheekbones. Eyes looking up. Two white earrings hung like un-melting snowflakes. In the center one was a star. In the other what looked like an upside down ‘Y’. Behind this black queen were red words. Power. To The. People. Books littered the top of her chest of drawers. She picked one up and the woman on the poster stared up from the cover. *Angela Davis: An Autobiography*, the title read.

“Come on,” her mother called. “Breakfast is nearly ready.”

Nadia sat up with a start. She got out of bed and walked over to the wall, timidly touching the book. Contraband. What was her mother thinking? She ran her finger over the image of the woman. She pressed her finger against it, and smiled as it bent at the first knuckle. She put her hand against it and pressed. Solid. She was awake.

Nadia looked at the door, which was slightly ajar. It suddenly opened and Nadia jumped.

"Easy girl! Come on, your eggs are getting cold," her mother said.

Nadia followed her mother into the dining room. She sat down at the old wooden table and looked at her plate. Fried eggs, bacon, toast. A heaping plate of hash browns in the middle of the table, next to another plate piled high with pancakes. Sliced cantaloupe heaped in a bowl. A glass of orange juice. Her mother set a mug of coffee beside the juice. Nadia had never seen so much food on the table.

"What's the occasion?" she asked.

"Occasion?" her mother answered. "Uh, Saturday morning?"

Nadia looked at her mother. Black curly hair stood out around her face, like the woman in the poster. Not like she remembered from the day before. She looked at her mother's face, her smooth brown skin. The corner of her mother's eyes, somehow not as …

"Wake up, Nadia. What's with you this morning? Still dreaming of handsome white boys with long blonde hair?"

"I dreamed he died," Nadia answered.

"Huh," her mother said. "That doesn't sound very nice. Eat your breakfast. Maybe he'll come back tonight," she said and smiled.

Nadia stared back. Slowly, she got up from the table and walked around the room. She walked to the mantel and picked up the framed picture of her father. He was smiling at the camera, or whoever was holding the camera. He looked happy. To one side of his picture was a framed print of a determined looking negro wearing a black suit and black framed glasses. He seemed to ooze confidence. And anger. On the other side sat an image of a man with a trimmed mustache. He had a softer, gentler face. Open and accepting.

"Who are they?" Nadia asked.

"Malcolm X and MLK Jr.?" her mother answered. "Are you still waking up?"

Nadia scanned the wall, searching for pictures of family members. Her mother with her hair sticking up. Nadia saw herself in a picture, in line with others, facing black clad police on a street she barely recognized. Her fist was raised. As was her hair. It looked like her mother's. She touched her own head and ran her fingers into a curly mass.

"That was a great shot, if I don't say so myself," she heard her mother say from the table. "Seeing as I took it. Are you OK?" she asked.

Nadia continued to scan the wall. There, in an old frame, was a black and white picture of a smiling woman with smooth brown skin, whom she had met one night and asked for help.

Nadia turned to her mother and pointed at the picture. "Ruby," she said.

"Yeah, that's right," her mother said slowly.

Nadia walked to the book shelf. It looked as if it had been a part of the wall for years, though it was the first time she had ever seen it. She scanned some titles. *The Wretched of the Earth. The Autobiography of Malcom X. If They Come Morning.* They were titles she had never heard of. Nadia picked one up. *When They Call You a Terrorist: A Black Lives Matter Memoir.* She held it up to her mother.

"What about the S-O?" she demanded.

"What's an S-O?" her mother asked.

"Security Officer. Cops. Police," Nadia said.

"What about the cops or police?" her mother answered. "Fuck the police, as the Niggers With Attitude sing. Sit down and eat. Quit acting so weird. You're starting to worry me."

Nadia put the book back and sat down again. The smell of bacon made her hungry despite her confusion. She picked up a piece and ate it.

"We're gonna do it, next week," her mother said. "They liked your idea. Close down Madison before a game, sit down and close off the whole street. Black Lives Matter out in glorious force, for all to see and take notice. There'll be plenty of cops, and plenty of cameras too, but cops behave better when they know they're being watched. We'll have our own body cams too, so ha! With this clown of a president the haters are really hating, but we got history on our side. Your friend from school still keen, what's her name? The big girl? Linda?"

"Linda," Nadia repeated.

"She's a good one to have beside you. Big. But you tell her, any trouble, just go limp and make them do the work. And just hold that picture of your dad nice and high so they can't forget what they done," her mother poured maple syrup over a stack of pancakes and cut into it.

"Here, have a read, you like to read when you eat, and it doesn't look like I'm gonna get much conversation out of you," her mother said, nudging a newspaper on the table.

Nadia picked it up and saw a picture of the president on the front page, the same orange clown that was usually on the front page. She read the headline, the first paragraphs. She read unfamiliar words. Scandal. Investigation. Impeachment.

Nadia turned and looked at the front door, solid and intact. She took some pancakes from the stack, poured syrup on them, added a piece of bacon as decoration. Thought for a moment and added another.

History is on our side. *Maybe,* Nadia thought. *At least it's different.* Smiling, she picked up her knife and fork.

Also by Christopher McMaster

Travel to the past (and alternate realities) with the next exciting books in the *Lucid* series: *Tomorrow's History*, and *Gods and Dreamers*

Travel to the future with exciting science fiction and climate fiction: *Misstep, Seeders, Pirates Come Down, The Nyrian Transmission* and *Journey to the Stars*

Tomorrow's History

LUCID, BOOK 2

*C*an one person *save a reality?*

London, present day. Airships pass overhead on their way north to the capital, Jorvik. Ships of the Great Fleet load at the busy docks, preparing for the voyage across the Western Ocean to the Far Settlements. The clang of Scandinavian steel still rings out and as you turn a corner, you're likely to bump into Odin, Thor, or Loki.

Jakob thinks his world is safe but it isn't. Something needs finishing for his present to come to pass, and he has been chosen to do it. The gods don't just stand by. Just as the sagas and the ancient stories tell, they like to interfere.

Trapped in waking dreams, he is thrust into an earlier age of Vikings, and into an adventure that can have only one outcome if his world is to survive.

Gods and Dreamers

LUCID, BOOK 3

*T*ime kills all things. Even the gods. That's why they interfere so much.

Three dreamers, manipulated by the gods to play with fate and shape reality. But as each becomes aware of their role, they are recruited into an unseen war, and taught how to fight back.

Together they struggle to protect their timelines and resist those that use mortals as their playthings. Each from a different reality, they must fight to protect what is theirs.

Only first they have to survive. There are others who think them heretics and will try to stop them at all costs.

MisStep

STEPPING, BOOK 1

Jens needed to get off the planet in a hurry so he took the first job on an interstellar freighter he found—part of a convoy to a far-flung mining colony, three Steps and almost three thousand lightyears away. Only the desperate went so far—colonists willing to trade a life on Earth for a new start on a rock somewhere across the galaxy, or spacers one step ahead of the law.

But as each Step takes him farther from home, Jens learns that the job isn't exactly what he was told, the cargo not as legitimate, and his situation even more precarious. Jens finds himself being groomed for a role in an interplanetary drug racket, with no way out.

Then the convoy mis-Steps, emerging lightyears off course, and the miscalculation might not be their fault!

Seeders

STEPPING, BOOK 2

A pandemic spread over their planet and swept them from history. In a desperate act to save their species they launched a remnant of survivors into the depths of space, frozen in cryo-sleep, to be awakened only when their ship detected a habitable planet. But there were no planets and the ship continued into the cold and dark.

Thousands of years later humans have settled the ocean world. Earth's dream of finding her sister planet has come true, and it was free for the taking. They gave it their own name, *Pemako*, and lived beside the ruins of what was once a mighty civilization. Picking through the artifacts, xeno-linquist Peter Taylor and a small research team find evidence of the Original's desperate mission. Plotting the probable course of the ship, the team locate where it might be, if it really exists, and if it is still operational.

The promised technology of the Originals outweighs any 'ifs'. But they need the help of a powerful earth-based consortia, as well as from Andrew Jensen, the only man to ever survive a confrontation with those whose planet they now call their own.

Pirates Come Down

A SOUTHERN OCEAN SAGA

Fishing in the future takes more than a net!

Rickets is a PAC-Man, his patrol and attack craft the first line of defence against encroaching vessels. Moss is a Fisheries Observer, tasked with ensuring companies abide by the quotas set on target species. Together they play a part in ensuring the waters are not fished to extinction.

But as fisheries elsewhere play out, New Zealand waters start to look more attractive until every ship protects itself with PAC boats, missiles that skim the surface, and kamikaze drones equipped with explosives.

Only there is a bigger shadow on the horizon, one that deflects all radar, is lethally armed, and takes what it wants!

The Nyrian Transmission

A SCIENCE FICTION LOVE STORY

After three hundred years of travelling across the expanse, it finally reached Earth.

The first signal was brief, and once deciphered consisted of three words: "Message to follow". The second signal took longer to decode, and was a detailed tutorial of an alien language. In the third transmission, the Nyrians introduced themselves.

In response, humanity sent two ships: The Concurrent mission travelled three hundred lightyears to see who was still there. The Response team folded both space *and* time to find out who originally sent it.

Both were unprepared for what they found.

Journey to the Stars

*S*cience *Fiction* Stories from the Bottom of the Ocean to the Depths of Space

An alien ethnographer collects death moments for his study. One Autumn morning he starts to show Chloe ...

A man's dream of meeting the lights he has seen in the sky, of journeying with them, turns to nightmare when he finally gets what he wants ...

With an asteroid hurtling towards the planet, a ship is sent to evacuate a colony. There are some that don't want to leave ...

In the early days of NASA, they thought the vast emptiness and solitude would be too much for the human mind to handle. For this space trucker, maybe they were right ...

And more! Eighteen science fiction stories from the bottom of the ocean to the depths of space. With a unique look behind the scenes in a conversation with the author.

To learn more about Christopher's books, visit him at:

www.christophermcmaster.com